To my frie

Mary

WOMAN OF SORROWS

A Historical Novel

Love Bev.

Beverly Lein

INKWATER
PRESS

PORTLAND • OREGON
INKWATERPRESS.COM

www.inkwaterpress.com

Paperback
ISBN-13 978-1-59299-608-7 | ISBN-10 1-59299-608-6

Kindle
ISBN-13 978-1-59299-609-4 | ISBN-10 1-59299-609-4

Publisher: Inkwater Press | www.inkwaterpress.com

Printed in the U.S.A.

All paper is acid free and meets all ANSI standards for archival quality paper.

1 3 5 7 9 10 8 6 4 2

I would like to dedicate this book to Bob Kulyna, Ozie Boos, Linda Hopkins and Mitch Gardecki.

People who left an imprint on those left behind.

I believe if they could tell us one more thing it would be to say, its not a bad thing to die.

Its just sad if you do not live while you have the chance.

Also a thank you to David the Friendly Editor and his knowledge of the Bible and who did the first drafts of the story.

Thank you to Dianne Smyth who spent many hours, editing and taking the story to the finish line.

A wonderful lady who opened her heart and mind to a new experience of letting the Lord in.

He kept her turning the pages.

To my Grandchildren, my stories, which will become there legacy.

Beverly Lein

Dear Reader

Please remember that this is a fictional love story. I do not want people believing for a moment that Paul and Mary Magdalene married. Clearly, that is *not* an historical nor a Biblical truth.

I hope that one day a woman becomes pope, and that she makes sure that every woman enjoys the same rights as men, the rights that Jesus Christ gave to all of us. After all, The Bible tells us that we are *all equal and* accountable for our sins.

Beverly Lein

MARY – WOMAN OF SORROWS

*J*oachim sighed as he laid a double offering at the temple altar — one for himself and his wife Anne — and one for the populace. The great Day of the Lord was at hand and the Sons of Israel were bringing their offerings. Joachim and his wife were up in age but he still carried himself with a stately grace. As he turned to leave, Rubin, a temple priest, approached and said, "Joachim, it is not proper for you to bring your offering."

Stunned, Joachim asked, "Why do you reproach me and say such a thing?"

Rubin, not wanting to hurt his friend's feelings said, "I am sorry, but you have not had a child in Israel."

Joachim was shocked. "I will seek council to see if this is so, for I cannot believe such a thing!" He made his way to the registrars of the Twelve Tribes of Israel, to see if he alone had not made seed in Israel. As he searched, he found that all the righteous he knew had indeed been blessed with children. God had blessed even Abraham, in his advanced years, when Isaac was born.

Joachim's heart broke. With he and Anne being so old, it was unlikely they would be blessed with a child. As he walked home he prayed and asked how he could please the

Lord God such that He would look on him with favour ... and bless them with a child. If Abraham could have a child in his old age, could it not happen for him and Anne?

Joachim did not go home to Anne. Instead, he retired to the desert, pitched his tent with his herd and his servants. There he fasted for forty days and nights, determining that prayer would be his food and drink until the Lord of Israel looked upon him with favour.

When Anne heard where Joachim had gone she walked to her garden and sat beneath a laurel bush, praying to the Lord, "Lord, hear my prayer. Bless me with a child and send my husband Joachim home. I am an old woman and need him by my side more than ever. If he is suffering, let us suffer together. I think he blames me for the lack of a child although he never says it out loud." Anne watched the sparrows flying back and forth to their nests. Tears flowed down her cheeks and she continued, "Even the birds are productive before you, O Lord, while I am barren."

A sudden rustle of wind made Anne look beside her and she saw an Angel of the Lord. A brilliant light emanated from him. Anne trembled and fell to her knees at his beauty. His wings were as white as his luminous garment. The angel said, "Anne, the Lord has heard your prayer and you shall bear a girl child who will be spoken of around the world. What you bring forth will be clean and without blemish."

Anne replied, "Whatever I bear I will dedicate to the Lord as a gift. May my child-to-be minister to the Lord in all holy things all the days of her life."

The angel nodded, saying, "Your husband will soon be home, for an angel has told him the news as well, the Lord

God has heard your prayer. The angel has told him to go home, to know you and you will conceive."

When Joachim heard the angel, he called his servants to bring twelve she lambs to be sacrificed. "They shall be for the Lord my God — without spot or blemish. Bring twelve tender calves, one for each of the Twelve Tribes of Israel. And bring one hundred goats for the priests and the people!"

Joachim hurried home to his wife and as he approached his home he saw Anne running to meet him. She threw herself into his arms and hastened to tell him the angel's message. Joachim hushed her by saying, "I too have seen an angel of the Lord! The childless shall conceive."

Nine months later the Lord God blessed Anne and Joachim with a girl they called Mary, which in Hebrew means "mistress of hope". Mary was a sweet child, and right from birth her Jewish bloodlines gave her a beauty beyond compare. With her dark brown hair, flashing black eyes, and gentle nature, those who knew her could not help but love her.

When Mary was one year old, Joachim held a great feast and invited the priests, scribes, elders, family, and friends. He reverently said, "O God of Israel! Bless this child and give her an everlasting name to be known in all generations to come." The priests also blessed her saying, "O God most high, bless her with the utmost blessings."

When Mary was three years of age Anne prepared to carry out their vow to the Lord to consecrate her to God. It was hard for Anne to leave her child at the temple with strangers. The little girl was frightened for she had never been without her mother. She cried when her mother left, even though Anne promised that every other week she would return to spend time with her.

Joachim, witnessing the heartbreaking scene, promised his daughter that he would come to see her on the days that her mother could not. The priest took the crying Mary from Anne's arms, kissed and blessed her. He tried to comfort the child, knowing it was a sad day for all of them. He sat her on the third step of the altar and the Lord God sent His comforting grace upon the child and she was comforted and waved to her departing parents.

In the temple was a special school for girls where Mary was taught handiwork as well as the Law of God. She prayed and read the scriptures for the next eleven years, growing into a deeply pious young woman. Each time Joachim came home from visiting Mary, his friends asked about her, and Joachim told them that the hands of angels were feeding Mary.

When Mary was ten years of age a two-year-old girl named Mary Magdalene was delivered to the temple by her family. She was extremely frightened at being alone until she was paired with Mary for protection and security. The older Mary loved her immediately, fascinated by little Mary's locks of black hair, which enhanced her black eyes and soft baby features. She not only slept and ate with the older girl but she followed her everywhere ... as though her life depended on it. At first, the little one cried frequently for her mother, especially at night. Mary, hearing her sobs, often crawled into bed with her and held her tightly, the little one clung fiercely to Mary. Often Mary felt so sorry for her that a lump would form in her throat and she thought, "This is one child who should be returned to her mother." Over the next four years Mary took on the role of the small child's mother and after some time little Mary quit being homesick. She even began to shy away from her own family when they visited, clinging fearfully to Mary until they left.

When the older Mary was fourteen, it was time for the priests to select a husband for her. They made preparations to send her home to her parents, Anne and Joachim. Great rejoicing filled their hearts and home as they readied themselves for her return.

But at the temple, Mary's heart broke at the thought of leaving little Mary Magdalene alone. Although the little one was only six she seemed to understand that Mary had to leave. But when Joachim and Anne came for their daughter, she asked if they would take the six-year-old Mary also.

Joachim replied that they would have to contact little Mary's family as they might want her back in her own home. Joachim approached the temple priests, stating that Mary was reluctant to go home with them if little Mary could not accompany her. About two weeks later word came from the little girl's family, stating that Mary Magdalene's mother had died, leaving the father to raise six other siblings. The father told the priests that he would be relieved if the child were to be raised by Joachim and Anne, as there was nothing more he could do for her.

As soon as she heard Mary told the little girl the good news, assuring her that she would not be leaving without her. So when Mary returned to her parents' home, she was accompanied by her acquired sister. Mary was very happy, for she had deeply feared that she would have had to leave the little girl behind.

Once the two Marys were gone, the priests at the temple discussed whom they should choose as a husband for the coming-of-age girl. The priest Rubin said, "Let us pray to ask what the Lord would have us do." As they prayed, an angel came to them and said, "Go out and assemble the single men of Israel and let them bring their staffs. Whomever God chooses will be made known to you with a sign."

The temple trumpet was then sounded to call forth the single men of Israel, and all the men within its sound knew it was a call to come to the temple for an important pronouncement. After the men were assembled, the priests went from one to the other ... but no sign was given ... until they came to Joseph, a widower with grown children. When they approached him, a dove came out of his staff and flew onto his head. Joseph, being quite alarmed, gasped, ... "What does this mean?"

Rubin calmly replied, "We have prayed concerning one of our virgins and you have been chosen to take her for your wife."

Joseph laughed and said, "I think not, for I am an old man of 40 seasons with grown-up children. I have no need of a wife."

The priest replied, "No Joseph, we have prayed and asked for a sign and the Lord God has chosen you. Do not scoff at what God has chosen lest you come to harm."

Joseph, being a God-fearing man, swallowed slowly and said, "Let it be so." He was then instructed to leave for Joachim's house to tell Joachim and Anne that he had been selected to marry their daughter.

As he approached Joachim's house, Joseph hesitated, preparing himself to tell Anne and Joachim that he, an old man, had been picked by the temple priests to be Mary's husband. Anne greeted Joseph cordially and invited him in. Even though he was past his prime it did not go unnoticed by Anne that Joseph was a handsome man with wide shoulders, gentle dark brown eyes, and a ready smile. "Anne," he said, "I have come to talk with you and Joachim."

Anne was honoured to receive Joseph as a guest, saying that she would call Joachim from the garden immediately. "He is getting old and does not leave the house much these days. He will be glad to have male company, besides the nattering of three women!"

When Anne left to get Joachim, a young girl of great beauty came into the room. Joseph quickly rose saying, "Hello, and who would you be?"

"I am Mary," the young girl replied, "the daughter of Anne and Joachim."

Joseph's felt a stab in his heart, thinking, "Are God and the priests all crazy to wish an old man like me on a young maiden like this one? What a waste of her young life ... the girl should marry one of my young sons ... not an old man like me. Life did not seem fair but Joseph knew that once the priests had spoken — it would be done — as they had ordered.

When Joachim and Anne returned from the garden, Mary politely bid Joseph goodbye and went outside. Joachim was most pleased to see his guest, saying, "Joseph, my old friend, what brings you here? Come, sit, Anne will get us a draught of wine while we discuss what business has brought you to our home."

Once seated, Joseph got right to the point and told Joachim what had taken place at the temple. Joachim was immediately saddened, for he had hoped a strong young man would be the husband of his child, certainly not his old friend Joseph. When Anne entered the room she knew instantly that something was amiss. She wondered what news Joachim had brought?

Her husband explained what Joseph had told him, unable to keep the disappointment from his voice. Anne cried, "Oh dear Joseph ... it is not that we do not like you but ... we had hoped for someone young and vibrant."

Joseph said, "I know Anne, but the Lord has picked me and the priests are in agreement that it must be done." Joachim and Anne knew the law. If the priests said it was so, it would be done.

Joseph continued, "I will marry your daughter, but because she is so young and because I have a daughter almost her age myself, I will leave her in your care for one more year. There is no rush to take her from her mother and this will give her time to mature and accept what is to be."

As Mary wandered in the garden with Mary Magdalene, she wondered out loud what the old man Joseph wanted. He appeared to be gracious and it had surprised her that he had taken time to speak with her. When Joseph left, she went back into the house, only to find her parents talking in hushed tones. Not wanting to disturb them, she was about to leave but Anne quietly said, "Mary, please come so we can talk."

"What is the matter Mother? You seem so sad. Has something happened?"

Anne nodded. "Yes child. Joseph has just come from the priests and they have chosen him to be your husband." Anne's voice choked with sobs.

Joachim put his arms around his wife. "Do not weep Anne. The law is the law and there is nothing we can do to change it. If God has spoken, it will be done. His plans are not ours and He must have a reason for picking Joseph."

Mary said, "Mother, maybe he is too old for me but I am sure he will be kind. I might have married someone younger, someone who might not treat me well. Joseph is not a rich man but neither is he poor. I am sure I will be well looked after. Do not fear, Mother."

Mary then went to her bedroom, putting on a brave front until she was out of her mother's sight. Once there she threw herself on her pallet and cried the tears of the frightened child she still was. She knew what would be expected of her as a wife and her innocent child's heart could not comprehend lying with a man forty years of age.

Soon, little Mary crawled into her big sister's pallet and wrapped her arms around her saying, "Please do not cry Mary. I will come with you."

⚭⚭⚭

Elizabeth rubbed her back as she set her husband Zachariah's supper on the table. She was of medium height with neatly coiled long dark hair. She was not a beautiful woman but there was something that drew people to her.

Zachariah said, "Is your back hurting again Elizabeth?" He stroked her hand as he settled slowly into his chair. Sighing, she sat on the opposite side of the table. Zachariah who truly loved his wife asked, "Why the heavy sigh woman? What is troubling you?"

"It is always the same," she said sadly. "My empty heart and body still yearn for a child. I have never quit wanting one and I never get over feeling guilty for not being able to have borne you a child," she sighed, "and I am now sixty-five. All hope is gone for having a child."

Zachariah smiled and said, "Hold your tongue wife you must know that what God gives, He gives and what He withholds, He withholds. For the first ten years of our married life I wanted a child, but for the past ten such thoughts have not come into my mind. I am set in my ways and a child would not be happy with old parents. Children need someone young to keep up with them. I would not have the energy to run after a little one and neither would you. Let us just enjoy the children around us; there are many others to love."

Elizabeth, who came from the tribe of Levi, had to agree. But Levite women were known for their ability to bear many children. Why could not she have been one of them? One woman could easily bear twelve children and she could not bring even one into the world. Zachariah got up from the table and Elizabeth hurried to the peg on the wall where his cloak hung. Helping him put it on she said, "I suppose you are very excited today?"

"Yes, my dear, I am." He had been chosen to fill the priest's office and according to custom, he was to burn the incense when he went to the table of the Lord in the temple.

When Zachariah arrived at the temple, the evening sacrifice was offered to the Lord. A young priest took fire from the altar of burnt offerings and handed it to Zachariah. Zechariah's eyes filled with a quiet joy for the task he was about to do as he followed the priest. Before entering the temple, the young man raised his hands. Silence fell over the crowd as the people prayed silently that God would accept their sacrifice. Their prayers and reverent silence would be held until Zechariah returned. He took the small box, entered the temple alone, and crossed the room lit by the burning lamps that hung along the walls. He went to pt.

the furthest side of the room. There hung a heavy veil in front of which was an altar with glowing coals. He opened the box and the scent of *stacte onycha*, made from a species of mussel which, when burnt, emitted a musky odour. The galbanum and pure frankincense was so overpowering that he held his breath.

He had to hurry for if he took too long, the people would think he had been struck dead for being unworthy to offer incense to the Lord. Zachariah sprinkled the spices on the coals and the smoke rose Heaven ward. He bowed toward the veil and as he straightened up, an angel of the Lord appeared at the right side of the altar.

The presence of the angel filled the temple with a light so bright that Zachariah's hands flew to his eyes. He had never seen anything so glorious and he flinched. The angel's outstretched wings and garments were as white as snow and the garments flowed as if a gentle breeze were blowing. The angel said, "Do not be afraid Zachariah, your prayers have been answered by the Lord."

"Prayers, what prayers?" The old man's mind was muddled because of the sudden appearance of the angel and he could not think. "What prayer?" Zachariah asked. "For I have prayed many prayers to the Lord."

The angel replied, "Your prayer for a child. Your wife Elizabeth will bear a son and you shall call his name John."

Zachariah smiled at the angel and said, "But we have ceased to pray that prayer, as we are now old and unable to have a child."

"Zachariah, you will receive joy and gladness and many people will rejoice with you at his birth. Your son will be a great prophet before the Lord. He shall not drink wine or strong drink. He will be filled with the Holy Spirit, even in his mother's womb, and will lead many of Israel to the Lord. He will go in the power of Elijah to prepare the people for the Lord."

Still trembling, Zachariah said, "How I shall do this, for I and my wife cannot conceive."

The angel replied, "I am Gabriel; my name means *stands in the presence of God Almighty* and He has sent me to give you these glad tidings. But because you did not believe, you shall be unable to speak until all these tidings come to pass."

As suddenly as the angel appeared, he disappeared, leaving only the lights of the lamps behind, taking his brilliant light with him. Zachariah hurried to the temple porch where the people were relieved to see him.

"Zachariah! We thought something happened to you!" Zachariah could not answer and they became anxious. "Did you have a vision?" someone asked. He nodded, gave the people a silent blessing and waved everyone away, for he could not ... despite his best efforts ... utter a sound. A friend got a paper and marker and Zachariah explained what had happened in the temple.

Once his term for temple duty was fulfilled, he returned to his wife. It was after these few days that she conceived. No one was more surprised than Zachariah when Elizabeth laid her head on the old man's chest and said, "I have conceived a child from the Lord. I am now able to fulfil my duty as a wife and give you, my husband, a child."

Anne mused as she remembered how Joachim always claimed that Mary was a very special child. He would often remind her that the hands of angels were fed her. Anne was thoroughly enjoying Mary being back home, for the years at the temple had been long for both of them. Mother and daughter enjoyed each other's company; more so because Mary knew that the time Joseph had allowed for her to become a woman would hurry by. So she clung to her mother as much as possible, dreading the day they would have to part again.

One afternoon when Mary returned from the garden to rest, a great light filled the room, and Gabriel, the Angel of the Lord, stood before her. His countenance was beautiful and gentle. He was dressed in a flowing white gown. Mary felt pure love radiating from the messenger. His great wings were spread, but as he spoke he folded them back. "Hail Mary! I am Gabriel. You are greatly favoured. The Lord is with you and blessed are you amongst women."

Mary fell to the floor, clenching her hands to her breast to still her pounding heart, "What greeting is this?" she wondered.

The angel told her not to fear. "Mary, you have found favour with God. You will conceive and you will have a son and you shall call Him Jesus."

The trembling Mary was trying so hard to understand what the angel was saying, but the thought kept rushing into her mind, "Is this really happening to me?"

"Yes, Mary," the angel said. "I am real and what you hear is the truth. Your son will be great and will be called the Son of the Most High. The Lord God will give to Him the throne of David and He shall reign over the house of Jacob forever, and of His kingdom there shall be no end."

The shining messenger was so convincing that, not even for a moment, did Mary doubt him once she decided that she was truly awake. But even with this assurance, Mary was confused and asked, "How can this be as I have no husband?"

Gabriel replied, "The Holy Ghost will overshadow you. Therefore, the holy being in your womb shall be born and shall be called the Son of God."

Mary's heart flooded with great joy when she realized that Gabriel must be talking about the promised Messiah — she was going to be the mother of the glorious Messiah! — He who had been promised to them for so many generations! Her thoughts were interrupted as the angel continued.

"Your mother's cousin Elizabeth was barren and she has conceived a son in her old age. She is now in her sixth month. Her son will be called John and he too shall be filled with the Holy Spirit, even from his mother's womb. All things are possible with God — nothing is impossible!"

Mary then calmly said, "So be it! Behold the handmaid of the Lord. Let it be done to me according to your word."

Gabriel nodded and smiled. He was pleased with Mary's answer — and just as suddenly as he had appeared — he departed, taking the brilliant light with him.

Mary slowly let her breath out and looked around her quiet room, still not sure that everything that had happened was real. A brilliant angel of great beauty had actually visited her! Tears filled her eyes as she pondered this great surprise and the angel's message. "So beautiful, so beautiful," she murmured. "I could have stayed with him all day. How much more glorious is God the Father?" she thought. "The elders always said no man could look upon God's glory and live." As she looked about her room, she wondered what to do and who to talk to about the angel's visit. Father and Mother? No. They would be horrified to know she was with child and might not believe her story. They would drag her to the temple, believing she had been possessed by the Devil. Suddenly she knew what to do. She would ask her mother if she could visit their kinswoman Elizabeth. If anyone would believe her, she knew it would be Elizabeth.

Mary hurried to the garden where Joachim was puttering with his vegetables. "Father, I wish to visit Elizabeth and Zachariah." Her heart was thumping as she waited for his reply. She wanted so much to share her news with him but did not know how. Joachim smiled at his much-adored daughter and said, "I do not see why not, but let us discuss this with your mother."

As they entered the house, Anne quietly asked, "What are you two up to?"

Joachim said, "Mary wants to visit Elizabeth. What do you think?"

Anne replied, "I think that would be good. Mary could help her around the house. Mary hugged her mother. She had made up her mind to tell her mother when Joachim left the house. There was no way she could be gone for three months and not talk to her mother about the angel and the great announcement. So, when Joachim left the house the next morning, Mary asked her mother to come to the garden with her. After her mother sat down, Mary said, "Mother, I have something to tell you but you must promise not to tell Father."

"What is it my child, that we cannot share with your father?"

Mary, already trembling and with her eyes closed as if in prayer, recounted the blessed event … "And that is why I want to go to Elizabeth's, for she is six months pregnant. I need her and she needs me."

Anne, stunned and shocked, said, "How do you know Elizabeth is six months with child?"

"The angel told me and he said her child is full of the Holy Spirit."

Anne sat with her hands clasped, knowing her daughter had been nowhere other than with her and Joachim. In all of Mary's years she had never spoken a lie, so Anne knew her daughter was telling the truth.

"So you will be the mother of the long-awaited Messiah ... Blessed are you, Mary ... " Anne whispered.

Mary threw herself into her mother's arms. "Thank you, Mother, for believing me!

"I had no choice but to believe you, for an angel once told me I was going to conceive a blessed child. That was *you*. I would have been deeply saddened if your father had not believed me, but an angel had spoken to him as well. Now we know why we were blessed with a child in our final years. I never could understand why we were given a daughter, not a son. Now I know you were picked to be the mother of the Messiah. Only a woman without blemish could be so blessed. Praise be to God.

Come child; let us pack your clothes and necessities for your journey to Elizabeth's. The sooner you can leave the better. We will tell your father when you return. I do not know that he or Joseph will believe this, but we will cross that hurdle when it is time. Since this only happened yesterday and you were home with me, I will mark the passing of days so no one can say you were somewhere else."

Anne was overjoyed with the news of Elizabeth's pregnancy. Anne knew how Elizabeth felt, for she had been barren until the Lord God had intervened. Not only that but Elizabeth and Zachariah were a lot older than she and Joachim. She was glad that they were letting Mary go to help Elizabeth and Zachariah out. Joachim would find out once he was there that Elizabeth was pregnant. To protect Mary she had to keep silent about Elizabeth's wonderful news.

Little Mary was sad she could not go with Mary to Elizabeth's but she was being spoiled by Joachim and Anna and enjoyed all the love and attention showered on her by the elderly couple. But somehow she sensed that Mary and Anna were hiding something from her. "Oh well," she thought, "they will tell me soon enough."

Joachim and Mary left Nazareth to travel south as fast as Mary could hasten her father. Joachim said, "Relax child. What is your hurry? Take your time and enjoy the trip to Judea." Each time they stopped to rest, Mary could not contain her happiness so she danced and sang. As she clapped her hands and laughed, Joachim watched his happy child and soon he was laughing and singing too. Her happiness was infectious and that was all Joachim's old heart wanted ... to know that his child was happy.

Once they reached Judea and Zachariah's house, Joachim told Mary to find Elizabeth while he went to the temple for a brief visit with Zachariah, his old friend, before leaving for home. He did not know how short the visit would be, since Zachariah still could not speak. Mary kissed her father goodbye and said "I will see you in three months, Father, when Elizabeth has a son." Joachim looked at Mary and said, "How are you so sure Elizabeth will bear a son?"

Mary caught herself and said with a gentle smile, that it would be nice for them to have a son. Joachim hugged his daughter saying, "Well my dear, they are pretty old to have children. "Goodbye my dear one" and took his leave, waving back as he saw Elizabeth coming out to meet Mary.

Elizabeth's first words were not those of a normal greeting. Instead, she burst out in praise. "Blessed are you amongst women and blessed is the fruit of thy womb!" Elizabeth instantly understood everything, for as soon as she heard Mary's voice, the baby in her own womb leapt, taking her breath away.

Mary said, "Elizabeth, then you know what has happened to me!" The old woman took Mary in her arms and hugged her. "Yes, yes, child, I know." Mary cried in her arms with relief.

Elizabeth said, "Blessed is the woman who believes that the Lord would keep His promise and these things will come to pass. Who believed God would keep His promise of a Messiah?"

Mary whispered. "Oh Elizabeth!" Mary could no longer contain her joy, "My soul magnifies the Lord. I am merely a maidservant before Him. My spirit rejoices in God my Saviour. I am nothing, but He looked down on me and He who is mighty has done a wonderful thing to me and I will henceforth be called blessed by all generations.

"He shows His strength with His arms and scatters the proud in the imagery of their hearts. The hungry and good are lifted up and the rich He sends away with empty hearts. God is helping Israel as He promised Abraham and all of his children forever. The Lord God keeps His promises."

After that memorable meeting, the two women, both carrying God's promises in their wombs, went into the house praising God; neither of them could put into words the pure joy in their hearts.

That night Mary lay in bed, happy that she could stay with Elizabeth and help the old woman. "At her age," she thought, "it would be hard for her to haul water or gather the fuel for the fire. It truly is a miracle for her to have a baby."

Mary's thoughts turned to her father and Joseph ... "How will I explain how I became pregnant? ... I am so glad that Mother and Elizabeth know but what will everyone else think? Will they think me a harlot? They probably will not believe an angel came to a simple handmaiden like me and that I have been picked to be the mother of the Messiah!" Mary turned over, pulled the blanket over her head and cried, not wanting the old people to hear. She was afraid, and as the night deepened and sleep did not come, she felt very much alone.

Mary worked hard for the next three months and got along well with Elizabeth and Zachariah, for they were a loving couple. Mary knew Elizabeth had told Zachariah about her carrying the promised Messiah, for when he walked by her; he squeezed her shoulder as if to comfort her. Not being able to speak made it hard for him to communicate and he cursed himself silently for doubting the angel Gabriel.

He loved having Mary to help Elizabeth, as she was kind and gentle, but he knew she was only going to be there until the baby arrived. He would have to get someone else to help Elizabeth once the baby was born. Zachariah often heard Mary crying in the night and knew that she was frightened. Unfortunately, all he could do was feel sorry for the young maiden, for when she would have to confront her father and Joseph. But, he thought, the Messiah was in the young woman's womb, right in his own home, and that made him very happy.

Three months later, news travelled through the town that Elizabeth was in labour and many gathered to await the birth of the child. Inside the house Elizabeth struggled as birthing pains wracked her body and Mary cringed every time she cried out.

Finally, after one strong push, the little one came into the world. The midwife handed the squirming baby to Mary, who wiped him clean. So this was birthing! Mary had heard a lot about having babies but this was the first time she had seen one come into the world. The infant was pleasing to look upon and, as Mary held him, her own baby moved for the first time in her womb. Mary stood still, wondering at the movement and Elizabeth asked, "What is wrong Mary?"

Tears filled Mary's eyes and she said, "I am so happy for you, and as I held your baby, my own child moved!"

Elizabeth nodded, "I know, child. I was overcome the first time my baby moved."

Mary finished wrapping the baby and as she handed the child to Elizabeth, both women's eyes filled with tears of joy.

Once Elizabeth was washed and the linen changed, Mary called Zachariah. He was overcome with emotion and the child was handed back and forth from father to mother to Mary and to the midwife. Elizabeth could not praise the Lord enough, thanking Him over and over, with Elizabeth speaking the words and Zachariah nodding agreement and approval.

On the eighth day, they came to circumcise the child. The child was circumcised at home with much talk and laughter, for all were happy for the old couple. As they began the ceremony, everyone assumed the boy would be named after his father.

"No," said Elizabeth, "his name shall be John." Shock filled the room and smiles stretched and froze as everyone spoke at once, trying to patronize the old woman. She had just had a child and surely was confused.

Mary stood beside Elizabeth, putting her arms around the old woman to protect her from the arguments that were already building in the room.

"Surely ..." someone said... "You want your son to be named after his father."

"Yes," exclaimed another, "it is the custom."

"He shall be called John," Elizabeth said again quietly.

All the smiles melted into stern-faced glares. "This is nonsense," the officiating priest declared. "Nobody in your family has the name John."

Elizabeth gently took her crying son from the priest's arms and repeated, "His name is John," and turned her back on the priests. "I have nothing further to say."

By now the impact of her words had sunk into the minds of the holy men and one of them said, "This is certainly no matter for women, we will speak to the child's father."

All eyes fell on Zachariah who simply motioned for a writing tablet. Once it was in his hands he wrote, "The child's name shall be John."

Mary's eyes, like those of both Elizabeth and Zachariah, filled with tears, as much from joy as from seeing the distress on the faces of their guests, most of whom were whispering among themselves, shaking heads about these strange goings on.

Elizabeth's face was radiant; she was not concerned about the fuss. The old woman took a deep breath and said quietly, "The Lord told us at the beginning the child's name would be John. When the Lord goes before you, how could we possibly do anything else?"

Suddenly, Zachariah started to speak, praising God. Everyone hushed as he told about the angel telling him he was going to be a father, how he had not believed, and that the angel had struck him mute. "The angel said the child was to be called John," he whispered, for his voice was not yet full strength. The people looked from the child to the father to the mother.

"Truly," a woman finally said, "something wonderful is happening for we can see that the hand of the Lord is upon this child."

Zachariah, suddenly moved by the Holy Spirit, fully understood what was to be. Gently taking the child from Mary, he said, "The Lord is remembering His promise to our father, Abraham. He delivered those who were without fear, those who loved and served Him, from the enemy."

Zachariah carefully lifted his son above his head and said, "This child will be a prophet of the Most High. He will go before the Lord to prepare His way, to give knowledge of salvation and to bring forgiveness of sin. This child will give light to those who sit in darkness, to those who walk under the shadow of death. He will guide their feet onto the way of peace."

Elizabeth took the baby from his father and handed him back to Mary. "It is time for us to rest. I am so very tired."

Mary's eyes widened as she began to realize what faced this baby who was filled with the Holy Spirit. She knew, intuitively, that he was to go ahead of her son, Jesus, to prepare the people to accept Him. Mary sensed that much sorrow was to come to the baby she held close to her.

Her heart was heavy as she laid him beside his mother to nurse. Their eyes met and without thinking, Elizabeth understood her thoughts and said, "Yes Mary, he will have much sorrow. For your child is the Son of God — and as cruel as the world will be to my son — one day yours will lay down His life."

Mary hung her head, unable to cope with thoughts of sorrow at such a joyous time. "Troubles, troubles, troubles," she thought. "What is coming to my child? Troubles even before He is born? I have never been so sad, nor have I ever cried so much."

Mary stayed another week before telling Elizabeth it was time for her to return home. It was time to tell her father and Joseph, and she prayed daily for the Lord to protect her and the baby under her heart.

She was well into her third month. Decisions had to be made. Mary readied herself for the journey, knowing she would greatly miss Elizabeth and the new baby boy with whom she had fallen completely in love with. How she would miss Elizabeth and her wisdom. "I wish I could take both of you home with me," she smiled. "I know we will see each other again, perhaps after my baby has come."

Anne, Joachim, and little Mary were overjoyed to see Mary. As she clung to her, little Mary cried, "I missed you so much! Three months was too long to be apart." They visited long into the night and talked of the blessed event of Elizabeth's new son and how he was named.

Two weeks passed before Mary had the nerve to talk to her father. As the sun started to set Mary said, "Father, I must share something with you." She explained the appearance of the angel Gabriel and his message, that she would be the mother of the long-awaited Messiah. "The angel also told me that Elizabeth would give birth to a son and that his name was to be John."

Joachim said nothing and Mary was frightened by his dark eyes and deep silence. But she bravely said, "Elizabeth and Zachariah have accepted fully that I am carrying the Son of God and their child will serve Him ... "

Joachim got up and walked to Mary. Before Anne could stop him, he slapped Mary's face and demanded, "Who is the father?"

Mary, holding her cheek and unable to hold back the tears, managed to say, "I am sorry you do not believe me but what I say is the truth."

Anne pushed between Mary and her father. "Joachim! We must talk!" But her words fell on deaf ears. He left, slamming the door with such force that a dish bounced off a shelf and fell to the floor. The smashing of the dish brought Mary and Anne back to the harsh reality of what had just happened. Holding her child, Anne said, "Come, let us get a cold cloth for your face."

Mary, sobbing heavily, followed her mother. Never had she been struck — and to be slapped by her father appalled her. She could not stop crying. "Oh Mother! He will tell Joseph!"

Anne said, "I suppose so but I will talk to your father when he comes home. He has done a great wrong here tonight."

When Joachim got to Joseph's dwelling he was exhausted. He could not believe he was at this man's house, carrying such a message, that he had to tell him Mary was pregnant with another man's child. He knew the betrothal had been destroyed.

Joseph greeted Joachim. "What brings you out so late, my old friend?" Joachim's heart broke as he told him of Mary's condition. Silence fell over them as Joseph pondered what to do.

He said, "I will not humiliate your daughter publicly. I will not allow her to become the laughing stock of the people." Joseph had not minded when Mary went to Elizabeth's alone. Neither had he minded that she was gone for three months, but somewhere, somehow, she must have met someone and fallen in love, probably someone younger, closer to her own age. "I was right the first time," thought the old man. "Nothing good can come from an old man marrying such a young woman."

Joseph paced the small room, thinking deeply. "Let us send her away," he said, "until the baby is born and we will tell the people I broke the betrothal because I felt she is too young for me. I will talk to her tomorrow and tell her what we will do."

Joachim, feeling very much like a broken old man, fell on Joseph's shoulder, loving him for his suggestion. "But how," he asked, "could my wonderful Mary do such a thing?"

Joseph said, "I need two witnesses to break the contract. The deed will be done tomorrow and that will end our problem."

Joachim took his leave of Joseph and slowly walked home, wishing he would never get there. What was left in life? His beloved daughter would be sent away, there would be no marriage, and no grandchildren. He and Anne would never know the child who was coming. "Why," he wondered, "has the Lord blessed me with a wonderful and good child like Mary, only to have this happen?"

His gaze drifted from the dark rocky path to the sky filled with stars. "Why did we let her go to Elizabeth's and why did you not look after her Lord?"

Mary laid waiting for her father to return. She knew Joseph had no choice. He must divorce her or send her away. Sorrow filled the young girl's heart for she knew it was going to be hard, but seeing her father fall apart had broken her heart. He, who was always kind and gentle, had been so provoked that he had raised his hand against her.

Mary knew that if her mother had not gotten between them he probably would have struck her again. The frightened crying girl finally fell asleep. She did not hear her father come in to look at her. Crying, he stroked the cheek he had struck, knowing he should not have hit her, no matter the reason.

As he turned around, Anne came in behind him and said, "Come, we have to talk."

When they were seated at the table, Anne said, "I should have told you about the angel. I knew about everything before Mary left to go to Elizabeth's. The angel Gabriel appeared to her the day before you took her to Elizabeth's. She did not want you to know. I noted the day when this took place so I *know* she is telling the truth, Joachim. She was with us all day before she left. You never gave me a chance to tell you that what she said was true. You got so angry, you frightened both of us!"

Joachim said, "Are you saying that she is carrying the child of the Lord, our *Messiah?*"

"Yes, Joachim, that is what I am saying. It is true. Did not an angel appear, telling us of Mary's coming? We always wondered why the Lord, if He was giving us a child, gave us a girl instead of a son. Do you not remember how we always wondered why we were so special that an angel would tell us we were going to finally have a child in our older years? Did not we wonder what kind of special child we would have? Has not she been the most wonderfully kind and gentle daughter anyone could ever want? Now we know why she was so special. She is going to be the mother of the coming Messiah!"

Joachim nodded tiredly and said, "I will do what I have to do and I will not let Joseph send her away. She is my daughter and I will look after and protect her myself." Joachim got up from his chair, went into Mary's room, and sat on the side of the pallet, lifting her into his arms.

"Papa, Papa," Mary murmured, "you are home. Thank God you are here. I was so worried about you. I am sorry, Papa ... but what I said is true."

Joachim wept as he said, "Mary, I believe you. I wish you had come to me from the start. I talked to Joseph and he wants to divorce you and send you away so as not to be embarrassed. But I will not allow you to be sent away, for you are my child and I will look after you. You are carrying the long-awaited Messiah and it would not be good to send away the long-awaited Promise. I am so sorry I struck you. Will you forgive me? I am so bull-headed! Why did I not listen to you? It is good you told your mother when you did for I still might not have believed you. You said Elizabeth and Zachariah believed you? Why did you tell them and not me?"

Mary said, "Papa ... when I met Elizabeth she already knew, for the Holy Spirit came over her."

Then Mary told her father and mother all that had been said and done while she was at Elizabeth's. They talked long into the night about what they would do and Joachim said, "If we have to move from here, so be it. But you will come to no harm as long as I draw breath."

Little Mary Magdalene, listening from behind her closed door, heaved a sigh of relief. She could not comprehend all that was being talked about but she knew something wonderful was going to happen to her Mary.

Closing her beautiful black eyes, she fell asleep on the floor and that is where Joachim found her. Picking her up and taking her to her bed, Joachim said, "I must have frightened you as well little one." Kissing her on the cheek, the old man lay her down on her bed, noticing that the child did not even stir.

Joseph lay awake, looking into the dark as if searching for something. If only he knew what had really happened to Mary. Maybe, if she had told him everything about who the father was, he might have kept her for his wife. He might have accepted the baby as his own to protect her. But she had been gone for three months and came home pregnant. People could count.

He would not have liked it had he married her and a child came three months early. That would have been a great betrayal, especially knowing that he had not touched her before marrying her. Yes, he had made the right choice but he could not understand why he felt so bad about it. He had not done the wrong she had, but still he felt ashamed and that he might be doing the wrong thing. Tossing and turning far into the night, Joseph finally fell into a fitful sleep.

And while he slept he had a dream. The room was suddenly filled with a magnificent light — and a messenger angel of great beauty stepped into his dream — "Joseph! I have a message for you from God. Do not fear taking Mary as your wife for that which is conceived in her is of the Holy Ghost and Mary shall bear a son. You will call Him Jesus and He shall save His people from their sins."

Joseph awoke with a start. The wondrous light that had filled his dream was gone. Now he understood what God was trying to tell him and that was why he had felt he was doing the wrong thing in sending her away. Perhaps it was also why he was feeling so badly about her father slapping her. Joseph leaped from bed knowing he had to go to Joachim's as quickly as possible to relay the angel's message.

He had to tell Joachim that he would take Mary as his wife and that what she conceived was holy. "There will be no sending her away, not now!" Joseph muttered. "I will fight Joachim if I have to."

As dawn filtered into his window, Joseph quickly dressed and threw on his cloak. As he picked up his walking staff, a dove emerged from the top of the staff and fluttered before him. Joseph heard these words, "You will be the earthly caregiver of Mary's child Jesus." Joseph bowed his head in joyous submission. And, before leaving for Mary's home, he knew he had to speak to some people in town.

Meanwhile, Mary dreaded getting up to face the day for she knew that the women of the town already suspected she was pregnant. She sensed they were discussing her as she walked by. Some shunned her completely when she greeted them, making her feel humiliated and rejected. She no longer knew whom her friends were and some of her young friends were already forbidden to talk to her.

Her bedroom door opened and her mother came in, "Mary, get up. Joseph is here and wants to talk to you." Anne reached out, hugged her daughter, and said, "We are here for you. Do not be afraid."

Mary dressed quickly and went to meet Joseph. "I have to know," she thought. "There is no sense prolonging the agony."

When Mary walked into the room, her father met her, and said to Joseph, "We will stand by our daughter and will allow no shame upon her."

Joseph smiled widely and said, "Joachim, you are so right! No shame will come upon this child. There is not going to be a divorce, no shame, nor sorrow put on her soul. Not another moment of it!"

He turned to look at Mary and said, "Gather your things, for I am taking you home to be my wife. I have prepared my house and friends and they are waiting for me to bring home my beautiful young wife."

Joachim and Anne were in shock; they could not believe what they were hearing.

Then Joseph told them about his dream and said, "God is fulfilling what He promised so long ago through the prophet Isaiah. Do you remember what the prophet said? I will quote it for you! 'A virgin shall conceive and bear a son and his name shall be called Emmanuel.' The virgin about to bear the Son of God is my Mary — and although His given name is to be Jesus, His whole being is "Emmanuel" meaning *God is with us*."

"Come now," Joseph said, taking Mary's arm, "We are going for a walk." Then Joachim followed through the town with Anne and little Mary. Joseph led the group, making a show of Mary, his new young wife, who now walked confidently by his side.

At the wedding feast three days later, he acknowledged everyone with grace and dignity. Mary was happy, for Joseph was always kind and respectful. She enjoyed his children, who, all but the youngest, were older than she was.

From then on Mary made sure to welcome Joseph's children whenever they came home to visit. And, since she was so young, they took to calling her their little mother.

❦

*M*ary was very close to her due date when a decree came from Caesar Augustus that their entire world was to be counted for taxation purposes. All citizens were ordered to return to the city or town they were born in for the census.

Joseph was very sad. He had no problem with going by himself but *everybody* had to leave. This included his pregnant wife. Mary could see he was upset about the decree and thinking about not going. She knew this would cause great trouble for Joseph's household, so she said, "If we start early and go slowly, we should be in time for the count."

Reluctantly, Joseph agreed and together they readied themselves for the long journey from Galilee out of Nazareth into Judea. From there they would go to the City of David, which was called Bethlehem, because he was of the house and lineage of David (and that meant Mary was too, because she had become Joseph's wife).

The journey was harder on Mary than she anticipated but she did not complain. Joseph had secured a donkey for her and sometimes she rode, other times she walked with Joseph.

They were about five or six hours from Bethlehem when Mary's back began to hurt and cramps began to ripple through her. "Joseph, I have no mother here to ask of these things, so being my husband I have to ask you something." Joseph nodded, so Mary quietly asked, "Do you have any idea what a birthing pain is supposed to feel like?"

The astonished look on Joseph's face made Mary laugh and she said, "Really, Joseph, I do not know what it is to give birth. I have a very upset stomach so maybe I ate something that did not agree with me and the cramps are getting worse. I do not know how much further I can travel."

Even though Mary knew nothing about the pain she was having, Joseph knew she was in labour. He knew all about delivering babies as he had delivered five out of six of his own. While delivering his sixth, things had gone horribly wrong and he had lost his wife. She delivered the baby, but haemorrhaged and there was no way to stop the bleeding. She died in his arms, leaving him with an infant and five very young children.

Joseph said, "Mary, you are having birthing cramps and they get harder and harder the nearer to birth you get. How long ago did these cramps start?"

"About four hours ago," Mary replied.

Joseph said, "We have about an hour-and-a-half to go before Bethlehem. Can you stand the pain until we get there so I can find lodging for you?"

Mary replied, "I will try. I do not want to have my baby out here in the dark."

They were about two miles from Bethlehem when Mary began to cry out. "Joseph! I can no longer ride on the beast." Joseph helped her down and as she started to slump to the ground, he picked her up in his strong arms and carried her.

It was late in the evening when Joseph entered the town. There were people everywhere, but at each place Joseph inquired for a room, he was told no rooms were available anywhere. He was desperate, for he knew Mary's time was very near. They came to yet another inn and Joseph said, "Do you have a room? Anything. We will take anything."

The innkeeper replied, "I am sorry, but there is nothing left." However, pity filled his heart as he looked at Joseph and the young woman in his arms. "If you are not fussy, I have a stable behind the inn.

My animals are in there but it is well kept and there is lots of clean hay for bedding." Mary heard Joseph say, "I will take it, for her time is very near."

The innkeeper called for his daughter and said, "Quickly, find your mother and tell her to come to the stable and bring what she will need to deliver a child." The innkeeper led Joseph and Mary to the stable. The night was very cold and he felt bad to have to put a labouring woman outside.

But when they entered, he noticed how comfortable the animals' body heat had made the stable. The innkeeper led Joseph to the clean hay and said, "My wife is coming to help. I will go and hurry her."

Joseph laid Mary on the bed of hay. She did not complain about her surroundings for she was glad to be off the road and out of the cold. "Joseph, bring me a blanket right away please," Mary said, crying out as another pain wracked her body. She pushed off her bottom clothes and covered herself with them until Joseph returned with the blanket.

Joseph had met the innkeeper's wife on his way to get the blanket. She was plain-looking woman with gentle brown eyes full of concern for the young woman lying in the hay. She'd brought water and clean cloths and hurried over to Mary, saying, "I will help your husband deliver the baby. I know it hurts, but try to take deep slow breaths when the pain comes. It will ease it."

It was a good thing that Mary had been with Elizabeth and was aware of the terrible pain before babies came. "How did that old woman," Mary wondered as another pain took over, "give birth and not die of the pain?"

The innkeeper's wife put another blanket down beside Mary, as she did not want the baby to fall into the straw. She hoped Joseph would hurry back before the baby came, as Mary had started to bear down.

Joseph rushed back with the other blanket just in time to grab the infant. Handing the baby to the innkeeper's wife he quickly tied the cord and the woman wrapped the shivering baby in the blanket.

Turning to Mary he cleaned her as well as he could and helped her back on with her clothes and cloak. Meanwhile, the innkeeper's wife cleaned the baby. Never had she felt such love and devotion for someone else's child. "How can this be?" she wondered, feeling confused.

She handed Him to His mother and as Mary wrapped Him in swaddling clothes and laid Him in a manger, she said, "Welcome to the world, Jesus Christ, Son of God." A sob caught in her throat — the King of Kings had just been born into probably the lowest estate in life — a stable full of animals.

Joseph said, "Mary, He will be fine and in a few days we will journey to my family home and visit there until you are strong enough to go back home."

Mary looked at her son. He was adorable and her heart filled with love as the age-old bonding that occurs when a woman gives birth. "How could anyone know what true love is until you hold your baby in your arms?" Mary thought.

She had always thought she knew what love was. She loved her parents and she loved God, but the Lord was going to be cross with her for she loved this baby more than anything in the world. And, as with most mothers, she knew in her heart that if her child ever came to harm, she would be willing to die for Him.

Mary decided the closest thing to God's love had to be a mother's love. No wonder mothers were so protective towards their young, for nothing in the world had prepared Mary for the overwhelming feeling of love she felt for this tiny boy child.

The night became colder and colder and the small group of shepherds shivered. Their little fire barely warmed their bodies but the light comforted them in the dark. They chatted about their wives and children as they watched their flocks sleeping in the cold of the night. One shepherd named Adam drew his cloak tighter as he gazed into the starry sky. It was a beautiful night, even if the cold penetrated their skin and they might be nearly frozen by morning. Adam had to laugh at his own humour. Mark, his friend, said, "What is so amusing, Adam?"

Adam said, "I was thinking how funny it would be if come morning we were all frozen to death. You know, just little mounds sitting up all stiff as wood."

His friend laughed at him and said, "You are one crazy man."

Suddenly a great light shone over the fields as an angel of the Lord came over them. The shepherds cowered in fear; they had never seen a light so bright or a being so beautiful. The golden light shining from the descending angel was almost blinding and they could not believe they were being visited by a Heavenly being. Things like this did not happen to simple people like them. What had they done to warrant a visit from the realm of God? They fell to the ground as if dead, wondering if they had done wrong and were going to be struck dead for their sins.

The angel said, "Fear not! Do not be afraid. You have done nothing wrong in the sight of the living God. I am Gabriel and I bring you great tidings of joy, which is for all people in all walks of life, including the rich and the poor. Unto you this day a baby has been born in the city of David, a Saviour who is Christ the Lord. You will find the baby wrapped in swaddling clothes and lying in a manger. The mother is named Mary."

The shepherds thought they had witnessed everything possible. Imagine! An angel appeared to them, but suddenly the night sky blossomed with a multitude of Heavenly hosts praising God and singing, "Glory to God in the highest and on earth peace and good will towards man." The shepherds stood with open mouths at the spectacular sight of the angels celebrating the birth of their King. There were so many that the shepherds could hardly contain themselves. The angels' joy was so great that the shepherds felt their radiating happiness as the feeling filled their souls. The beauty of the Heavenly singing was so wonderful that tears ran down the men's faces. Forgotten was the cold night as they cried and wrapped their arms around one another. The grandeur of the radiant light from the Heavenly bodies could not be explained. Slowly the Heavenly multitudes started to disappear, still singing their beautiful song as they went back to Heaven. Gabriel was the last to go, saying once more, "Peace on earth! Good will towards men!" As they watched him go higher and higher, his light became dimmer and dimmer until it disappeared in the depths of the dark starry sky.

The shepherds turned to one another and Mark exclaimed, "Did what happen really happen?"

Josh said, "I saw a great angel called Gabriel and a multitude of angels singing, and they were all so magnificent I cried like a baby."

Adam said quietly, "We all saw the same thing so it was no dream and if I die tomorrow I will die a happy man. How wonderful that lowly ones like us saw some of the wonders of Heaven! I want to go and see the long-awaited Messiah."

Mark said, "Come, let us all go to Bethlehem to see this birth that the Lord has made known to us."

As they headed into Bethlehem, the starry night was quiet and beautiful, healing their hearts as each one thought of what he had seen and heard. Leaving their flocks alone, for none wanted to miss the great event foretold by the angel, they trusted in the Lord to keep the flocks safe until their return.

As they neared the place where the angel had told them to go, a luminous cloud overshadowed the stable. Josh said, "My heart is at wonder because my eyes have seen strange things. Salvation has been brought forth in Israel." Immediately, the cloud disappeared from the stable and a great light shone inside so brightly that their eyes could not bear it. The great light began to decrease as they entered the stable and as they hesitated in the doorway, wondering what to do, Mary motioned to them. "Mary? Are you Mary?" asked Josh.

"Yes I am," said Mary. "Why do you ask?"

"We have seen Gabriel, the angel of the Lord, and a vast multitude of singing angels celebrating the birth of the new King. He told us how to find this stable and that the baby's mother's name is Mary."

Mary pondered the men's words in her heart. She simply knew she had to remember these wonderful things that were happening concerning her child. She picked up Jesus and handed Him to Josh and said, "This child is to be our Saviour, yours and mine. Hold Him and remember Him."

The roughly dressed shepherd held the child closely, weeping as he looked at the babe. The baby's black eyes looked straight into his soul and a deep peace filled the man's heart, a peace he had never felt before. For the first time in his life he did not feel fear or the worry of how to feed his family. He just felt peace. Josh passed the child to Mark, who gave Him to Adam until all had held the child. They too wept as if their hearts were broken. When the last of the rough men had held the child, he said, "I cry as if my heart is broken. But yet I feel such peace and happiness. I do not understand what is wrong with me." All the men nodded in agreement and looked at Mary to see if she had an answer.

"Love," she said quietly. "You have all felt the miracle of love and peace tonight. Your lives are hard and the everyday worry of being taxed to death and working for so little has been your bread. Now the Lord God has sent you one who will care deeply for you. All you will have to do is ask for love and protection from Him.

The child was passed back to Mary who, through her tears, looked at the raw emotion etched deeply in the faces of the shepherds. "Yes," she thought, "they will take the great news of the new King and tell everyone what has transpired this wondrous night."

The promise from God had been fulfilled and they could not wait to take the news to everyone they could find. They bid Mary and Joseph goodbye, then went straight to the inn and told everyone about the glorious angels and what they had been told concerning the child.

The shepherds, returning to their flocks in the early morning dawn, were tired and still praising God for the blessing of being the first to see the King of Israel. And until their dying days they talked about the beauty and the splendour of the angels announcing the birth of the King.

After the shepherds left, Mary put her son in the manger and leaned against Joseph who was sitting beside her. "What does it all mean Joseph?" she asked. "What lies ahead for this baby?"

Joseph smiled and said, "Probably many wonderful things. Just look at the celebration of the angels. I wish we had seen it too."

Mary closed her eyes and thought, "I must remember all these wonderful things. I will ask Joseph to keep them for me."

When the eighth day arrived, the child was circumcised and His name was given. It was the name Jesus given to the child by the angel Gabriel before He was conceived.

After six weeks, it was time to take Jesus to Jerusalem to present Him to the Lord, for it is written that every male child that opens the womb shall be called Holy to the Lord. Mary was feeling well and the journey was not hard on her or the baby. When they reached the temple, Joseph said, "What do you want for the sacrifice, a pair of turtle doves or two young pigeons?" Mary picked the turtle doves, and when they entered the temple they met an old man named Simeon, a just and devout man. It had been revealed to him by the Holy Ghost that he would not die before he had seen the face of the Lord's Christ. When Simeon saw Jesus, he was moved by the Holy Spirit and his heart leapt in his chest. Hardly daring to breathe, he said to Mary, "Woman, is the child yours?" Mary nodded and Simeon said, "May I hold the child?"

Mary placed the baby in his arms saying, "Of course you may."

He lifted the baby into the air and blessed God and said, "Lord, I now can depart in peace from this world. My eyes have seen Thy salvation, the Saviour of the world." Weeping, Simeon said to Mary, "Woman, long ago I was promised by the Holy Spirit that I would not die until I had seen the Christ of God. I have been waiting all these years for this child, the light of the Gentiles and the glory of the people of Israel."

Simeon blessed Mary and Joseph and said to Mary, "Mother of the Christ, many shall argue for Him and many will be against Him. Hatred will be in many of the arguments surrounding Him for He will have the power to look into people's hearts. Whoever shall fall on this stone shall be broken but on whomever it shall fall, it will grind them to powder. A sword shall pierce your soul as you go through your life with your child. Yes a sword shall pierce through your own soul also so that the thoughts of many hearts may be revealed." Simeon blessed them again, told them goodbye, and disappeared into the crowd.

Mary whispered, "What a dear sweet old man. May God bless him."

They performed the rites as prescribed by the law and, when they were done, made their way back to Bethlehem. Mary was quiet on the journey and with it being late; she went to bed, taking the child with her. Joseph could hear Mary crying in the night but he did not want to intrude on her thoughts and feelings for he knew the day had given them so much. Any prophesizing was never good where their son was concerned, for it seemed many would harm Him if they could.

Mary held her child tightly. He was so little, so helpless. How could she protect and shield Him from a hurtful world? She prayed to God the Father to give her strength, for she sensed she had much to endure.

Jesus was over a year old when Three Magi from the east appeared. They had travelled far, following the star that appeared when He was born. Their journey was long and tedious, but the star never faded as they followed it. By the time they had organized their caravan and servants, much time had passed, but the star kept shining brightly as if to say it was waiting for them.

When they arrived in Jerusalem they asked, "Where is He who is born King of the Jews? We saw His star in the east and have come to worship Him."

King Herod was outraged when he heard of their questions, but invited the Magi to his palace. Barely containing his fury as they were ushered into his throne room, he asked where the new King was supposed to have been born. They conversed amongst themselves, thinking how strange that this king did not know where the child was born or that one so great had arrived into the world. He did not even know of the prophecy concerning the child's birth.

They said, "In Bethlehem of Judea, and the prophecy says that out of Judea shall come a governor who will rule Israel." Herod asked how much time had passed and when the star first appeared. They told him much time had passed and that now they were anxious to be on their way.

Herod said, "So be it! Go and search for the child and when you have found Him, send me word so I too may come and worship."

They left the king's presence saying to one another, "There is something not quite right about that man." The oldest Magi said, "I never want to lay eyes on him again. He is pure evil."

As the Magi left the city it was already evening. Never had the star shone so brightly. The star they had followed so far from the east went before them until it stood over the house where the young child dwelled.

Joseph greeted them. He was deeply impressed by their great importance, for never had he seen men dressed in such splendour. "Come and rest," he exclaimed. "You look like you have travelled a long way. Our home is humble, but you are welcome."

The Magi, stiff and sore from their long journey, introduced themselves, saying that they had seen the child's star and it had led them here. Joseph took them into Mary where she was holding the King. Immediately they fell to their knees, worshiping the child. Mary could not believe the wonder of God — it had taken these Wise Men almost a year-and-a-half to find them and she marvelled that God had brought three kings so far to worship the King of Kings. There was no jealousy amongst the Magi because before them was a greater king and they were happy to know the chosen one had arrived. The Magi had their servants unpack the camels, bringing Jesus gifts of gold, frankincense, and myrrh. Mary was taken aback, having never seen such gifts. "Joseph? Can we accept these gifts?"

"Yes Mary. They are not for you or me but for the Son of God." The Magi nodded at Joseph's words, seeing him as a good and wise man.

Mary made a meal for the three and offered them their hospitality for the night. They gladly accepted as it meant they could spend more time with the little King. They knew that once they left they would never see Him again and their hearts mourned that fact.

As they slept that night, God warned each of them in a dream that they should not return to Herod but go back to their country another way. The evil king did not want to worship the child but meant Him great harm. In the morning the amazed Magi talked over their dreams, only to find that, word for word, they had been given the same warning. When Joseph got up, they told him of their dreams and warned Joseph that Herod meant only to harm the child. Joseph said, "I will be careful and try to protect Him from Herod." Joseph watched them depart until they were out of sight. He had greatly enjoyed these wise men, but his soul was deeply troubled about their dreams and their dire warning.

Beverly Lein

As Joseph slept that night, an Angel of the Lord appeared in all his splendour and beauty. "Joseph," he commanded, "get up and take the child and his mother. Flee to Egypt and stay there until I bring you word. Herod seeks to destroy the child."

Herod flew into a rage when he found out the Magi had avoided him by returning to their country by a different way. He sent his soldiers into Bethlehem, ordering them to slay every male child who was under two years of age.

Before death and destruction descended, Joseph had obeyed the Angel of the Lord. He quickly woke Mary and said, "Hurry! Get up and get dressed. Pack what you can for clothes and food. I was warned in a dream to take you and the child and escape into Egypt." Mary shook the sleep from her head, got out of bed, and immediately started packing their few belongings. "But who would want to hurt the child?" she wondered.

Joseph said quietly, "Herod is coming. There can only be one king and it is going to be him if he has any say over the situation. He will destroy the child if he gets his hands on Him."

Fear for her child flooded Mary's heart as she gathered their things. "Is this what it is going to be like all my life?" she thought, looking at the sleeping child. "Will we always be filled with fear?" Tears coursed down her cheeks. She could not comprehend that someone would deliberately kill such innocence. Once ready, Joseph took Mary and Jesus into the cold night — and started the long trek to distant Egypt —and safety.

As dawn was breaking, just hours after Joseph had fled with his family, soldiers rode into Bethlehem. With ruthless efficiency, they broke into homes, grabbing babies from their mothers' arms and putting them to death. Parents who fought for their children died beside them. The blood-bath lasted for hours and there were dead babies every-where. As the soldiers rode out of Bethlehem, the screams of the mothers rang in their ears. After Bethlehem, they continued their campaign of terror in the surrounding dis-tricts, leaving more screams to fill the air and more blood to stain the streets and soak the dry sands. Many a hardened soldier wept, for never had an order from the king been so brutal, so horrendous. But they were soldiers. And if they disobeyed it meant death.

The prophecy of Jeremiah the prophet came true, that in Rama there was a voice heard of Rachel weeping and wailing for her children. And Rachel could not be com-forted, for the children were no more.

Elizabeth, hearing they were searching for the babies in her district, took her baby John and went into the hillside country. She tried to find a place to conceal herself and the boy, but could not find anything suitable. Moaning in fear, she pleaded, "O mountain of God, receive mother and child, for if they find the baby they will kill him." Immediately, an opening was cleft into the rock concealing them and a light shone around them, for an angel of the Lord had come to protect them.

When the soldiers came to the temple and found Zachariah, they demanded, "Where have you hidden your son! We know you have a boy for it is in the census. Where is he?"

Zachariah said, "I am a servant of the Lord in holy things. I sit constantly in the Temple of God and I do not know where my son is. If I did know, I would not say, for you have killed all the babies in our country. What you have done is wickedness! You have shed innocent blood for a madman." A soldier drew his sword and rammed it through Zachariah's heart. As the old man fell to the floor, he cried out to the Lord, "Protect my son O holy Father! Save him from the evil of these wicked men."

When the news of the massacre reached Egypt, people were horrified at what Herod had done in his kingdom. The Pharaoh of Egypt said, "I am not always a just man but if I had one wish, it would be that this king dies a terrible death."

Mary wept for days after hearing of the deaths of all those children, many of whom she knew as friends and family. Many died so her child could live and one day she wondered aloud to Joseph, "Why was the whole country not warned so they also could have hidden their children?" Joseph knew not what to say, but God opened Mary's heart so she could begin to understand what the prophecies meant. Many had died so that her child could live, and someday die, so all could be saved from their sins. Mary wondered if Herod and his soldiers would ever be forgiven for the violence they had inflicted on the children.

No, Herod would not be forgiven, for he was as Satan, considering himself higher than God. It was not long before news of Herod's impending death filtered out to Egypt saying that the evil king was dying a long and painful death. He had lived such a life of debauchery that worms infected his flesh and were eating him alive. His flesh rotted and fell from his body and he cried out for death. His enemies were full of glee. Nowhere was there any pity for this demented man. The Pharaoh of Egypt remarked, "I do not always get what I ask for from the gods, but this time they granted my wish."

When Herod died, Joseph asked Mary if she wanted to return to Bethlehem, but Mary was too afraid of Herod's son. He ruled in Judea and was as evil as his father. Mary said, "Let us go home to Nazareth in Galilee and raise the child there. Mother and Father are getting older and need me. They must be worried about our safety and what has happened to us. Little Mary needs me as well and I miss her. I have not seen her or my parents for two years.

That night the Angel of the Lord again appeared to Joseph, saying that Mary's wishes were good ones, and that the child would be safe in Galilee.

There was great rejoicing when Mary and Joseph returned to their home in Galilee. Anne and Joachim finally had their grandson home safe and sound after so many had died. And until they laid their eyes on Mary and the child, they had no way of knowing their love ones had survived the great massacre. Little Mary Magdalene was nine when she first saw the boy Jesus, who was by then two years old. She was immediately smitten with the beautiful little boy with His piercing black eyes. There was something so endearing about the child, and even at two, there was a seriousness about Him that made Him look older than His age. Mary Magdalene spent all her free time with Mary and Jesus and when Joachim died a year later, Anne and little Mary came to live with Mary and Joseph.

Mary was a wonderful mother, teaching Jesus and Little Mary the Jewish faith of the one living God. She taught them to pray for the poor and the enslaved Hebrews, to bring them into their covenant relationship with God. Mary and Joseph practised their Jewish religion in their home, followed the Torah, observed the Sabbath and the festivals, recited prayers, lit candles, and went to the synagogue according to the customs in Galilee.

Mary's life was now also full with Joseph's older children: James, Jose, Simon, Judas, Rebecca, and Leah. Mary was young for a stepmother, but Joseph's children loved her. Mary tried hard to fill the place of their mother. She was always gentle and fair and she quickly found a warm place in their hearts. Joseph's children were all older than Mary except for Judas the baby, who was one year younger. The family adored their baby brother Jesus and protected His secret of extraordinary powers. They were in awe of Him, for He told stories of God His Father and of angels in Heaven. Looking and listening to the innocent little boy when He told His stories, they were of one accord that they would protect the child until He was old and wise enough to know what to say in front of people. They knew that someday Jesus was to minister to the world ... and until then He had to be protected. The family knew of His birth, for Joseph had told them of his disbelief until the time that the angel appeared.

Mary rubbed her aching back. It seemed that no matter how hard she worked she was never done. Everybody had jobs but it seemed to Mary that each day brought more work than the day before, and there was never enough money. It was not that Joseph did not provide for them, but they were always struggling under the triple taxation of the temple, Herod, and Rome.

Mary was Jewish through and through and whenever the opportunity arose she told Jesus and little Mary about the announcement from the angel Gabriel concerning Jesus. When little Mary heard the story, her heart overflowed and she would pick up the little boy and hug and kiss Him.

He would squirm to get free, squealing with delight and loving the attention. Mary and little Mary noted that there was something special about the child, for He performed miracles at an early age.

Joseph, being a carpenter, kept Jesus close to him, teaching Him the trade. Joseph and Mary were astounded at the child's knowledge and wisdom and how the grace of God was so evident and so abundant upon Him.

*J*esus was very excited; for His mother had told him they were getting ready for the Passover journey to Jerusalem. He had just had his twelfth birthday and was feeling quite grown up. They would make the journey with others from the village. He knew it was always a fun time, for there was little work other than packing water and taking care of the animals. Mary prepared food for the journey that did not take a lot of time to cook. And that meant He would have lots of spare time to play with His friends. When the family was fully organized, they left early one morning. Anne, Mary's mother, who was old and increasingly feeble, needed more help than usual and Joseph did not want to make the journey harder on her by rushing.

Mary Magdalene had just turned nineteen and Mary had a birthday celebration for her during the journey. She was now a stunningly beautiful young lady with ebony hair that fell to her waist. Mary smiled to herself as she watched little Mary finish the stitching on a cloak she was making. Mary Magdalene's father had arranged a marriage for his daughter and it was to take place after the Passover. Mary and Joseph were very happy about the arrangement, because her father had picked a handsome young man. Joseph was especially happy, for he never liked it when old men were picked to marry young girls. He believed that young people should marry young people.

Mary was happy that Mary Magdalene's father had been in no rush to marry off his daughter. Usually, young girls were married between twelve and fourteen years of age, so Mary Magdalene was considered old for marriage at nineteen. Mary and Joseph never let it bother them that she was unmarried. They just loved having her with them. Jesus and Mary Magdalene were very close and Mary knew that when little Mary left them to live in Magdala with her husband Jesus was going to be lost without her.

Once they reached Jerusalem, Mary and Joseph let Jesus go here and there as He pleased. There was so much to see and do and the boy was excited to see everything all at once. Mary Magdalene followed Him everywhere, making sure He did not get lost or wander too far. When the days of the Passover were fulfilled, Mary and Joseph left for home with the rest of the village caravan. Mary had been enjoying visits with the other women, discussing children and husbands, but when night fell she went to find Jesus to put Him to bed.

Joseph was having a good time in the company of the men when Mary approached. "Joseph, could you call Jesus to come? It is late and time for bed."

Joseph stared at Mary and said quietly, so as not to frighten her, "He is not with me. I thought He was with you."

Mary was frightened as they searched for their son amongst family and friends, but none had seen Him. She whispered, "Joseph, what do you think has happened to Him? I am frightened!"

Joseph replied, "We must return to Jerusalem. He probably got lost and we did not know it. Mary Magdalene can look after your mother and make sure all is well with her. Rebecca and Leah can help. The boys can help too, but we must hurry back. Let us not wait for morning, we should leave now."

In Jerusalem they searched everywhere but could not find Him. Mary, remembering all too well what King Herod had done, worried that something terrible had happened, that the past had caught up to her son. "How could I have been so careless!" she accused herself over and over.

For three days they searched. Finally, they found Him deep in the temple, sitting in the midst of doctors and scholars of the Law, listening and asking questions. He talked with such wisdom they were astonished. Mary was so happy to see Him that she wept.

Then she shook Him by the shoulder and scolded Him in front of the amused scholars. "How could you disappear without telling us where you were going? We have been trying to find you for three days and we looked *everywhere*. We could not sleep because we were sure something terrible had happened to you.

Jesus replied, "Mother, why were you looking for me? Did you not know that I must be about My Father's business and be in His house?"

Mary and Joseph did not understand. And at the time they thought Jesus was treating them harshly. After they returned to Nazareth, Mary thought many times about her son's words and his deeds, and she knew then that she must keep them in her heart. She watched as He grew in wisdom and stature, finding favour with God and the people.

∝∞∾

There was great excitement as Mary Magdalene's wedding day approached. Her family had come to Nazareth for the wedding. And the day before the wedding Mary had met her husband-to-be for the first time.

Jacob was a strong, good-looking young man and there was an immediate attraction between them. Mary knew that little Mary was going to be very happy with her young man. Jacob was pleasant, a bit on the serious side, but he had a way of teasing that added to his attraction. Mary Magdalene, on the other hand, was shy and reserved, but once she knew and trusted someone, she had a loving and giving nature that made people want her as their best friend.

The wedding was a beautiful affair, but too soon it was over and the bride and groom were packed and ready to head back to Magdala. The two Marys cried, hating to part, for they had been together since Mary Magdalene was only two years old.

Jesus came running to Mary Magdalene, and when she saw Him she cried even harder. She hated to leave this young man she loved so much, wondering who would He confide in once she was gone They had shared many secrets about who He was and the holy things that only He could perform and talk about. She loved to listen to Him speak of God, the angels, and of the Heaven He called home. She did not always understand the things He said but she never doubted who He truly was.

Three months after little Mary's wedding, Anne passed away in her sleep. Mary was distraught, for she loved her mother so much. Jesus was upset at the loss of His grandmother, for they too had been very close. But Anne had lived a long life and was, as she had once told her daughter, ready for her eternal home. She had recently said, "I have lived a good long life but I keep getting more and more tired with each day. It is time that I go." Mary smiled as she remembered her mother's words. She had not realized it would come so soon.

Mary had just gotten used to her mother's passing when Joseph, her beloved protector and husband, died. He'd never had a sexual relationship with Mary, as he always felt God's presence around her and he deemed her holy. Joseph always had a clear comprehension of Mary's great morality, eminence, humility, as well as her faith, obedience, and dedication to God. Over the years, he had always been conscious of her deep devotion to her divine son.

He never forgot the angel's words of her being worthy, meaning that she had attained favour from God. Joseph also realized that Mary had a prophetic vocation with God as He had placed her in the key position as His partner in bringing about the birth of the Messiah.

It had never bothered Joseph not to have relations with his young wife, for he had never desired her in that manner — he loved her as a daughter, not as a woman. There had been one woman in Joseph's life that he had loved and had children by, and that one romantic love was enough for a lifetime. Besides, the angel had told him he was the earthly caregiver of Jesus and Mary. He had taken it to mean just that, a caregiver to one who belonged to someone else, a special person who belonged only to God.

As Joseph lay dying, Mary said to him, "You have been such a good man and husband. I always felt loved and safe with you."

Joseph said, "You have been a good woman, loving and accepting of my children and taking care of me and my home. There will be hard years ahead for you, but trust God to bring you through. Soon it will be Jesus' time to minister to the world. You know He can perform miracles for we have both seen His strength and courage. But the day will come when you have to face the world with Him and the mockery that will come with His time. Do not be afraid, Mary, and do not forget that you are the Mother of Christ the King!" The children gathered around and Mary held Joseph to her breast as he passed from life into death. The children comforted her as they laid their father to rest.

Some time later, word came from Magdala that Mary Magdalene had given birth to a girl they called Rebecca, named after her good friend Joseph's daughter. Three years later she gave birth to Sarah.

Mary travelled once a year to Magdala, with Jesus, to visit young Mary and her family. Never had Mary seen such a loving and happy family. They were a joy to be around. She and Jesus usually stayed about a week, getting reacquainted with the children. The two close friends, Mary Magdalene and Jesus, spent much time visiting each other while Mary looked on. Mary always enjoyed her visits with her stepsister and there always were sad goodbyes each time they parted.

By now Elizabeth was very old and frail but Mary loved to spend time with her. She still had a quick wit that made

Jesus laugh at her jokes. John, Elizabeth's son, often smiled lovingly at his aging mother and said things like, "I wish I had known her when she was young."

While Mary and Elizabeth visited, John and Jesus spent a great deal of time together talking. John was fully devoted to Jesus and wise beyond his years. Mary still felt a great love for the young man. She remembered him as a baby and had always known that he was destined to go ahead of her son and prepare the way for Him.

The years flew by after Elizabeth passed away and Jesus and John no longer saw each other as often. When Jesus was around the age of twenty-eight, news came from Magdala by a messenger. A terrible accident had taken Jacob and the girls. The little girls were playing by a well when one of them decided to crawl into the bucket. Rebecca was supposed to lower the bucket with Sarah in it then wind her back up. But the heavy bucket fell into the deep well and Rebecca was jerked over the side with it. Jacob saw what was happening and hollered at Mary to run for help. Without thinking of his own safety, he leaped into the well. By the time help came, all three had drowned. As they lifted the bodies from the well, Mary was hysterical — screaming and struggling — desperate to jump into the well to join them in death.

After that incident Mary Magdalene quickly sank into a deep depression, not eating or responding to anybody. She did not care if she lived or died. No one could reach her for she refused to talk to anyone. She talked incessantly to herself as she wandered around the village, as if looking for her loved ones.

Mary mourned the loss of Mary Magdalene's family and wished that she had been there to help her cope with the loss of her loved ones.

Then, one day Mary Magdalene just disappeared. No one knew where she had gone. The assumption was that she had wandered into the desert and had leapt from a cliff.

*J*esus came to his mother one day saying, "Mother, John the Baptist is at the River Jordan baptizing people and telling them the Kingdom of God is at hand and to repent of their sins." Mary's heart skipped a beat. She looked into her son's eyes as He said, "I must go to the river to be baptized. I want you to come with me, for my Ministry is about to begin." Mary walked with her son to the River Jordan; with her heart beating so hard she could scarcely breathe. She knew, intuitively, that many things would soon come to pass and this was only the beginning.

As they approached the river they heard John the Baptist saying, "I am the voice crying in the wilderness. Make straight the way of the Lord. I baptize with water but there is one standing in your midst whose sandals I am unworthy to tie! He will baptize you with the Holy Spirit and with fire." When John saw Mary and recognized her, he said, "Welcome, Mary. Have you brought your son to me?"

Mary nodded and said, "He is here but He has brought me with Him." As she spoke, the serious young man walked up to John, put his hand on John's shoulder and said, "Baptize me."

John could barely breathe, as he said, "No! I should be baptized by you, for You are the living Word."

Jesus then replied, "Come John, and baptize me, for it is up to us to fulfill all righteousness. Let it be done."

So John followed Jesus into the water and baptized Him. As Jesus emerged from the water, the Heavens opened and the Spirit of God descended like a dove and a great light hovered around Him. A voice from Heaven said, "This is my beloved Son in whom I am well pleased."

Mary thought her heart was going to burst wide open with fear, pride, and happiness when she heard that great voice from Heaven. She could hardly believe what she was hearing and seeing. She watched Jesus pull his tunic over His body, then reach out to John.

They hugged and John said, "I finally found you after all these years. I have waited for this moment, for this is why I was born." Jesus looked at John — a strange sight — dressed in camel hair and a leather girdle about his loins. The only food that touched his lips was locusts and honey. But one had only to listen to him to know he was filled with the Holy Ghost and that his raiment and what he ate was of no importance to him. His only thought, his only deed, his only purpose in life, was to prepare the way for the King of Kings now standing in the water in front of him.

Mary waited until the men were done talking, then she said, "John, please baptize me as well." John looked at her and said, "I would be honoured to baptize the mother of my Lord." Mary waded into the water and John baptized her as Jesus held her hand. Mary watched Jesus walk away from her, wondering out loud where He was going. John said, "He is going into the desert to fast and will be gone for forty days and forty nights. He will be tempted by the Devil."

"Oh no, John. Do not let Him go. He will be in great danger. Please stop Him for me."

John said, "No Mary. This He has to do. His hand will purge His floor and gather His wheat into the granary but He will burn up the chaff with unquenchable fire. He has to fight the Devil so Satan knows the Lord God cannot be tempted."

Mary looked at John as if he had completely lost his mind. What he had said did not make sense. John took Mary into his arms saying, "Come, I will explain all to you."

The Devil did his best to tempt the Lord until Jesus had had enough and said, "Get away Satan, for it is written, 'You shall not tempt the Lord your God and Him only, shall you serve.'"

The Devil departed and angels came and ministered to Him with food and drink.

When Jesus returned home after the temptation, Mary was aghast at the state her son was in. His body was thin, haggard, and He limped on bloodied feet. Gently, she helped Him to His bed and nursed Him until He was well. While He recuperated, He told Mary how the Devil had tempted Him three times and how great and terrible the power of the tempter was. "Mother, never underestimate the enemy ... " He said, " ... For he comes only to kill and destroy all who love God the Father."

When Jesus regained his strength, Mary often went with Him, to observe His great power. They met Simon, Peter, and Andrew and Jesus said, "Come! Follow me and I will make you fishers of men." Mary marvelled at how they immediately left their nets to follow, even though their fathers were hollering after them, "Where are you going? There is work to be done!" They turned to wave and called out, "We are going to follow Jesus!"

James and John were mending nets with their father when Jesus called them. They too left their father and followed. Then came Philip, Bartholomew, Thomas, Matthew, James, Judas (the brother of James), Simon, and Judas Iscariot.

Mary, who had travelled with her son as He picked out His apostles, marvelled at their faith in Jesus. They left everything familiar to follow him. She knew in her heart that a great divine intervention must have been taking place for the men to do what they were doing. None of them would have left parents, wives, work, and children if God did not have His mighty hand in the whole situation.

Mary and Jesus were invited to a wedding in Cana. Mary came early and Jesus and the disciples a little later. The wedding feast was truly lovely but when Mary noted that her hosts were upset, she said to the mother of the bride, "What is the matter, Jana?"

"Mary, we have run out of wine and the evening has just begun."

Mary nodded and said, "I will find Jesus. Maybe He can help."

Mary approached Jesus, who was talking with the men in the garden, and whispered, "Son, they have no wine left."

Jesus was well acquainted with her kind nature toward others, but He also knew she was asking Him to use His power to perform a miracle. He answered cryptically and said, "What is it to me, woman? My time has not yet come."

Mary smiled lovingly at her son and was not discouraged, as she was confident that He would not ignore her plea. She turned to the servants and said softly, "Whatever He tells you to do ... do it."

There were six stone water pots in the corner and Jesus said to the servants, "Fill the water pots to the brim." With this done, Jesus told them to draw out some of the water and take it to the wedding feast.

When the host tasted the water, now changed into wine, he did not know where it had come from. But the servants knew and later told him what had happened. They knew they had just witnessed a miracle.

The guests said, "At most weddings the good wine is brought first and when men have drunk well, the lesser wine is brought out. But these hosts have saved the best wine for last!"

The apostles marvelled at this miracle, but knew full well that Jesus had just manifested His glory to them and they believed in Him even more. But never again did Mary ask Jesus to perform a miracle for her. It wasn't that she doubted Him or thought He would deny her, but she realized that it was up to Jesus to decide when and where a miracle would be performed.

Mary followed Jesus and listened to His teachings. She loved the compassion He showed for sinners, for lepers, and for those who were possessed by demons. Of all He healed, those who were possessed frightened Mary the most for they were very powerful and extremely violent. The demons fought Jesus with great power because they would not easily surrender any soul over which they had control. She listened to the praise and love the people gave her Son and her heart filled with gladness.

But when she heard mockery and belittling from the unbelievers and the sceptics, she could not hide her sorrow and keen disappointment. She could not believe that a people who had waited centuries for a Saviour could not and would not accept the Chosen One when He stood in their midst.

Jesus, His mother, and the apostles travelled to the coast of Caesarea Philippi, with Jesus teaching and healing as they went. One afternoon they went out to the high cliffs and hills of Caesarea where there were many caves and caverns. Jesus wanted to spend some quiet time with His apostles and thought the surrounding area was a comforting place.

As they walked toward one of the caves, a wild-looking woman with billowing black hair came screaming toward them hollering, "Jesus Christ! We know who you are! Let us be. Let us be!"

Mary fell to the ground in a dead faint, for the wild-looking woman in tattered rags and foaming at the mouth was none other than Mary Magdalene. Filth poured from her mouth as she cursed Jesus and the confused apostles.

John reached down to help Mary from the ground as the commotion around them intensified. The woman flew at Jesus, trying to scratch His face. She had superhuman strength as she grappled with Him, but Jesus held her wrists and said, "Satan! Be gone!"

A harsh guttural voice issued from the woman and it said, "There are seven of us. There is a herd of swine, let us depart with all of them. Do not send us to the pit!"

And Jesus said, "Let it be done."

As the seven demons burst out of Mary Magdalene, she fell to the ground as though she were dead. The demons, entering the swine, caused them to run over a cliff to the sea below. Jesus stooped over and with John's help, lifted the poor woman to a sitting position.

She was light in His arms for she was little more than a bag of bones. The townspeople used to bring food to this desolate place once in a while for they knew of the crazed woman and felt compassion for her. No one knew where she had come from and for years, no one could help her. They were surprised she had remained alive this long for they had seen her do many terrible things to herself.

By now Mary had gotten her wits about her and went to the demented being lying on the ground. She dabbed at Mary Magdalene's face with a wet cloth but the woman remained unconscious. "Jesus," Mary said. "Quick. We need a fire to make broth. I must get some food into her."

"Mother," Jesus said, "she will not die because she sleeps the very deep sleep of healing. The broth will be ready when she awakes but for now cover her and let her rest."

"Oh Jesus," Mary wept, "how did this happen?"

Jesus helped His mother up and said, "When Mary lost her family, and she became so depressed it was easy for demons to overwhelm her. She lost all faith and had no will to live.

Remember her people saying she talked to herself and not to them before she disappeared? The evil ones had taken over her body and they drove her to madness, forcing her to go where they wanted. They kept her alive just enough for a dwelling. They found it gleeful to take over a soul that at one time was a child of God. When she became weak and lost all resistance they attacked and they won."

Mary made the broth and sat by her younger sister, lifting Mary Magdalene's head to her lap. Looking at her dirty and scratched face one could not see the beautiful girl of long ago. Her feet, legs, arms, and every part of her body Mary could see, festered with poorly healed or open wounds.

Mary gently washed Mary Magdalene's face and when she woke, it was to see her older sister holding her head in her lap. Mary said, "How are you are feeling my child? Do you want something to eat?" Mary Magdalene nodded. It was all she could do because her throat hurt such that she could not talk. The demons, in making her constantly scream, had all but stolen her voice.

Once Mary Magdalene had eaten she fell into a deep sleep. Mary watched the still form sleeping ... barely breathing ... barely alive. It had been a long time since she had been free of the demons. Mary thought that Mary Magdalene hovered near death, but she was wrong. The younger woman slept deeply till the next afternoon when she awoke Mary fed her again before helping her up.

They went to a stream where Mary bathed her little sister and washed her long matted hair. Mary cried as her eyes fell on Mary Magdalene's naked torso. There was not a place where her skin was not bruised, scratched, scarred, or broken open. Mary said, "Child! Do you remember anything you did while you were possessed?"

"No, no," she whispered hoarsely, "I ... "

"If you do not want to talk just now ... " started Mary.

"I can talk," sighed Mary Magdalene. "I can only remember trying to find myself back there. That is all I remember. I was lost in my own body and I ... I ... could ... not get out," she stammered, near to tears.

As Mary rinsed the younger woman's hair, she said, "Mary, I have to cut your hair."

Mary Magdalene put her hands to her head and said, "Oh ... No Mary! Can you not brush out the tangles?"

Mary said, "No child, it is too tangled. Take my comb and try. You will see it is impossible. I have to cut it for you."

Mary Magdalene tried a brush, then a comb, and finally said, "You are right. It must be cut off."

Mary used shears to cut Mary's hair, leaving it about two inches long. As the matted and dirty hair fell away, Mary Magdalene shook with sobs and Mary said, "Child, you can keep your head covered until your hair grows back."

"It is not my hair," Mary Magdalene said, "I am thinking about my husband and how he loved to brush my long hair at night." Mary hugged her sister and said, "Why could not I have been there for you?"

All afternoon they sat by the stream while Mary Magdalene poured out her heart, recalling how her children had died, how she had held them in her arms until the people came to bury them. "I screamed and fought," she recalled, shuddering at the memory of having her little ones pried from her arms for the last time.

She barely remembered the funeral, with her family carrying her at times because she was so grief stricken. "Somebody told me losing a loved one shuts down part of the body," Mary Magdalene said. "When I lost my girls and my husband, I think my heart shut down. I was completely numb, just numb. I could not eat. I could not sleep. I do not remember anything.

All I could think of was my children never being fed again, lying like dolls in their graves. I did not want to live.

I heard people talking but their voices faded and gradually they became further and further away. I do not remember leaving my home. I remember someone trying to feed me, refusing to eat, and than being told that if I did not eat I would die. I remembering thinking what did it matter if I died, that's what I wanted to do.

As evening fell Mary said, "Come, let us join the others for supper. Jesus is probably wishing we would come so He can talk to you. He did not bother us in the afternoon for He knew there was much for us to discuss. He will be anxious to see you."

Mary Magdalene said, "When I woke to see Jesus standing over me, I felt my body had been pulled apart from the inside."

Mary nodded, "The demons did not want to leave, so they hung on inside. They would have ripped you apart if Jesus had not cast them out."

As they reached the apostles, Jesus greeted them, taking Mary Magdalene in His arms; he kissed her face and said, "How you have suffered my sister."

Crying, Mary Magdalene hugged Him and said, "Thank You, Jesus, for freeing me. I am free —I am free at last!"

Jesus replied, "We were told you had committed suicide but I knew that not to be the truth.

After they ate, Mary Magdalene asked Jesus, "How did the demons get such control over me?"

He answered, "They got to you because of your weakened state. You were no longer praying and you thought God had disappeared along with your babies. These thoughts made you vulnerable to satanic attack. Remember Mary, we must pray without ceasing, for we are not dealing with people of the earth but with the darkest hordes of hell."

John brought bowls of food for the women. Thanking him, they ate silently, thinking of the great miracle of change that had happened before their eyes. Once the meal was finished, they visited long into the night, for they all wanted to hear everything that Mary could remember. There was not a dry eye amongst the men as she told of the loss of her husband and children. Or how she survived through the demonic possession for over two years, she did not know, but God had interceded. "I know I have my soul back," Mary Magdalene smiled, "and I have so much to live for.

After that Mary and Mary Magdeline travelled almost everywhere with Jesus and the apostles. Young Mary began her work having been blessed by Jesus to heal, cast out devils, teach others, and anoint the dead and dying. She became the thirteenth apostle. Mary worked mostly with women and children, but if she knew Jesus was teaching somewhere, she would hurry from home to home to announce that he was nearby.

Many times Mary travelled with Mary Magdalene to help, for the harvest was never-ending. And there were broken hearts, broken dreams, and shattered lives everywhere, for life was very hard.

One evening she approached Jesus, telling Him she was weary and wanted to go home for a while. Jesus said, "Yes, Mother. Go and rest, for you have been with me a long time, never leaving my side. I know what is in your heart, Mother. You think if you leave my side, like when I was a little boy in the temple in Jerusalem, that you cannot protect me. Mother ... Mother ... All things in their own time will come to pass and for all your worrying you cannot change the future." Hugging his mother He lovingly said, "Go now. I will come to no harm. I need some rest, and we are going to get a boat so I can sleep for a while." And they went their separate ways, Jesus to the seashore, and Mary back to her home.

The sky was black with huge thunderclouds and a strong wind. Mary hoped the men would not go out too far. She arrived home just in time to escape the storm's fury. As the rain fell in great sheets, she made her supper and hoped Mary Magdalene would be back home to eat soon. The two women still shared the little house and still loved being together. It was nice to lock out the world at night and rest in peace, far from the commotion of her son's teachings and healings.

Mary Magdalene's body had mended quickly under Mary's care and she was as happy as she could be. She now lived for Jesus, truly believing Him to be the Son of God. She had never doubted His identity as some of His followers did from time to time. Where she had been and the things she had done in her two years of possession slowly came to light.

People who had fed her had also taken the time to watch her actions, as she had often climbed high rocks as though intending to kill herself. Whenever anyone approached her, she had screamed and raved, spouting the vilest of curses, and threatening to kill them. They had occasionally restrained her but she always broke free, snapping the bindings like threads. It had taken six men to hold her and nothing would calm her. They thought if they could restrain her they could at least feed and wash her, and prevent her from hurting herself. Finally, they gave up ... they left her to her own devices ... to live or to die.

As Mary Magdalene hurried through the door soaking wet, chased by the growing strength of the storm, Mary greeted her, "Hurry and change and come to the table, supper is ready." Mary, busying herself with the food, smiled as she glanced at the younger woman, for she was very happy to have her back home.

Mary Magdalene's joy at her new life was evident on her face and in everything she did. Through Jesus' grace she had been saved. She felt clean inside and out ... no longer spending endless hours weeping for her lost family. She dedicated herself to Mary and Jesus. Helping with His teachings was all she lived for.

The next morning when Mary got up, Mary Magdalene was already gone. "What a woman, she never quits!" Mary thought as she made breakfast for herself. As she sat there eating, Peter knocked at the door.

"Peter! What brings you here so early?"

"Mary!" he exclaimed with his usual enthusiasm, "I have something wonderful to tell you."

"Come in Peter, I am just having some breakfast. You must join me and tell me your good news."

As Mary prepared an additional breakfast, Peter said, "After you left us at the seashore last night, the crowd surrounded us. We tried to go, but they wanted to hear more and more from Jesus. Somehow Jesus slipped away and we got to the boat. Strange thing though ... when we were loading Jesus was not there ... but the crowd followed us, thinking He was with us. We had no choice but to leave the shore without him. There were so many people grabbing at us, they could easily have capsized us.

Once we were away from shore, that big storm moved in with full fury. The wind howled and lashed at the boat and our sails. The waves must have been at least ten feet high and we fought to keep the boat from tipping. The storm was frightening but we became more afraid when James said, 'Look! What is that?' Through the waves we could see a dim light floating on the water. It was coming toward us.

"Someone yelled, 'Who is it'. Mary, we thought it was a ghost! We did not know what it was. Shuddering in our boots, we thought the end had come. But suddenly the light took on the shape of a man and when he spoke, our hearts nearly failed us."

"Do not be afraid. "It is I.""

"Mary — you will never believe this —it was Jesus!"

"Really?" said Mary. "You were that close to the shore in a storm?"

"No! No Mary. We were in the *middle of the sea* and Jesus was walking on the water. He hollered to us above the wind and the waves. I could not hear Him well and thought I had to help Him, so I stood up and stepped over the side of the boat and started to go to Him. He said, 'Come Peter!' and held out His hand. Without a thought, I was — I was — *walking* on top of the water, just like Him. But suddenly the waves and the wind made me afraid and I began to sink. I remember yelling, 'Lord! Save me!' He reached down into the water, caught me, and said, 'Oh Peter, of little faith. Why did you doubt?' I was so sad because I had failed Him and doubted Him — but of a truth, Mary — He surely is the Son of God!"

Mary walked over to Peter and gave the big man a hug. He crumbled into her arms and said with tears in his eyes, "Am I *always* going to doubt Him?"

Mary whispered and said, "Even if you do, He loves you and will forgive you."

❧

It was almost a month later that the disciples went fishing and another storm caught them. Jesus, who had fallen asleep in the boat, was unaware the waves were about to swamp them. So great was the storm, that they woke Him yelling, "Lord save us! We are going to drown!"

Jesus stood up and said to the wind, the waves, and the rain, "Be still!" And the waves disappeared, along with the rain and the wind. He turned to His open-mouthed apostles and again said, "O you of little faith! … "

As Mary heard about these miracles and others, she gradually was able to let go of her Son. She had always known He was the Son of God but a part of her had held on to that little boy. Now, whatever happened, He would have to take care of Himself and his followers.

Around that time, the Lord God made known to Mary through a visitation of the angel Gabriel, what was about to come. He said, "Many will follow Him and believe in Him as their Saviour … and many will not." He explained how and why Jesus was going to die and the suffering He would endure. He said, "Your suffering, as well, will be great, but you must endure for His sake. Before Jesus," the angel said, "there was no hope for mankind but with Jesus dying for our sins, all who accept Him will be saved."

Mary wept as the angel unravelled the future for her and she whispered, "My poor son."

The angel replied, "Mary, Jesus knows what is to come and has known ever since He was a child. He knows He will die and in three days be raised up. Jesus, as the Son of God, is being given as the sacrificial lamb and he has much to endure. God will put His Spirit over you, so you can bear what is to come." With those words, the beautiful shining angel left Mary, trembling and alone with her thoughts.

Mary went to find Jesus and found Him in Bethany at the house of Simon the leper. As she entered the room, a beautiful woman was pouring precious ointment on the head of Jesus. Mary recognized her as the woman the people had been about to stone for adultery. Jesus had stood by her, asking the crowd what she had done. They told Him her sin was adultery and Jesus said, "He who is without sin can cast the first stone."

Some of the disciples murmured amongst themselves at the waste of the expensive ointment. Jesus rebuked them saying, "The poor you will always have with you but you will not always have me. This woman has poured the ointment on my body for my burial. I tell you this ... wherever the gospel is preached in the whole world it will be told what this woman has done ... and it will be a memorial to her. For much she has been forgiven and for much she loves the Forgiver."

As He said this, He looked up and saw His mother. "Mother," he said, standing to greet her. They looked into each other's eyes and Jesus said, "You know what is to befall me. The angel has appeared to you."

Tears fell from Mary's eyes, "Yes, it has been revealed to me" ... sobbing ... she entered His arms and He held her close.

Mary and Jesus were terribly upset to hear that the cruel King Herod had beheaded John the Baptist. Herod's wife hated John because John called them on the murder of Herod's brother. Herod and his brother's wife had carried on their adultery right under the brother's nose while he was alive.

The queen also knew that the king found her daughter, Salome, attractive. One evening the girl danced for the king and he told her she could have whatever she wished. On her mother's bidding, she asked for the head of John the Baptist on a silver platter.

Mary and Jesus wept, for their dear friend would be sadly missed.

Mary and Mary Magdalene noticed that, as people loved Jesus more and more, so grew the hatred of the chief priests. Mary knew she could no longer protect Him.

When someone made disparaging remarks about her son she would quickly mention His good points ... healing the sick and the curing the lepers ... and His love for all people. She often said to Mary Magdalene, "How can they be so blind?"

Mary Magdalene knew Mary's heart was sad for she was not herself. Mary finally confided in Mary Magdalene what the angel had told her. Mary Magdalene, who was truly shocked, said, "How can this be?"

He was their Saviour, but as Mary explained, Mary Magdalene slowly began to understand. Her thoughts wandered to when Jesus was little and how much she had loved Him. She had just turned seven when He was born and thought at first not to like Him. After all, Mary belonged to her, but now she would have to share Mary with this baby. But what actually happened, when Mary Magdalene got to know Jesus as a little boy, was love. She had loved Him as a baby and she loved everything about the man He had become. To face the certainty of losing Him now was a burden on her soul.

One day the two Marys were at a home helping to deliver a baby being born to a girl barely fourteen. Mary Magdalene said to Mary, "I hate this so much. These are just babies having babies." Mary nodded and said, "I know. It bothers me too. If I had a daughter I would never allow one so young to marry."

As they went home, Mary Magdalene said, "Mary, I think we are being followed."

"Do you think they mean us harm?" Mary asked.

"I do not know," Mary Magdalene said, "but just up ahead there is a little turn-off. We can hide in there and see who it is."

As they waited to see who was following them, Mary was thinking, "We should have kept going ahead. We should not be confronting someone out here."

Her worries and protests were silenced as a well-dressed woman walked past. Without thinking, Mary Magdalene jumped out behind her and demanded, "Why are you following us? Who are you?"

The young woman was of great beauty and her attire had certainly come from a rich man's coffers. "I am Salome, niece of Herod the King."

"Are you lost? We can help you find your way back to your home."

"No," Salome said. "I can never go back. I am looking for the man they call Jesus. I was told that you are His mother and the other one is His aunt? I was following the two of you, hoping you would lead me to Him."

Mary replied, "We are almost at my home, so come. We will talk there."

Once settled inside the warm little home and with water for tea boiling, the two Marys waited patiently for Salome's story.

"My father was King Phillip, but Herod, who is my uncle, and my mother were having an affair. They plotted to kill my father, but Herod, who then became king, was no better than my father had been. My mother had great plans for her future, with me being one of them. I have always done what she told me, right down to asking for the head of John the Baptist. But now I have to refuse my uncle's demands that I sleep with him.

My mother thinks there is nothing wrong with this and ordered me to do it. But now she has become terribly jealous of the attention bestowed on me by the King. My mother does not care what happens to me. She never has. I heard her telling one of her maids that maybe once he has had me, I will no longer interest him.

One day I heard a fascinating man teaching on the street. It touched my soul because nothing in my life had ever made me as happy as I was in that moment. I listened to the teacher and thought about my life and all the evil things I had done. He told the people that these things should not be done! He talked of salvation and sins being forgiven. I *want* that in my life!

Not just once in a while when it is convenient but all the time. I want to know about and listen to more of His teachings and I want it as if the other me had never existed. I want to take off my finery and ask you to find me some-thing to wear that is more like your clothing. I want to look like you and be the same as you, for I do not want to be found by the King or my mother. I desperately want to follow this man Jesus.

I truly believe He is the Son of God. John the Baptist believed in Him, and now I do to. I want to make up for my role in what happened to John the Baptist. I want to learn and to preach the gospel Jesus teaches. Maybe then I can live with myself and ask for the Christ to forgive my sins."

The two Mary's listened in astonishment and when Salome finished, Mary Magdalene said, "You poor little thing. Come. We will get rid of this finery and throw it in the river. If anyone from Herod's court finds the clothes, they will think you are dead and no one will bother looking for you. If your mother is as cruel and heartless as you say, she will not come looking for you, she will just be thankful you are out of her way. Indeed, you shall meet Jesus and He will forgive you, because you sinned before you knew Him."

When the apostles were introduced to Salome, there was much murmuring amongst them. Finally they picked James to speak to Jesus for them. "Lord, we have great con-cerns. We are happy that You have forgiven Salome her sins. We do not care that she eats our bread. We will share everything we have with her. But Lord, how can we trust her when she brought about John's death? We know much about where our people hide. How do we know who she really is, inside? Maybe she will tire of our ways and betray the people who trust us."

Jesus smiled gently. "Do not be angry with her. If you were threatened as she has been, you do not know what you would do. Remember, if she betrays us and our people, what would we do?" The apostles did not know so Jesus said quietly, "We would have to forgive her, is that not right?"

They nodded satisfied with His answer … for love and forgiveness is what Jesus taught. They accepted His words, for this man wanted them to love their enemies, feed the poor, heal the sick, and love one another as He had so abundantly loved them.

The time was nearing for her son to suffer. Mary knew it was coming but she did not know when.

When it was time for the Passover Jesus said to Peter, "Take John, go into the city, and prepare the Passover supper. While you are there, bring my Mother, Mary Magdalene, as well as Salome. I want my mother near me tonight. We will all eat together."

Peter and John went to Mary's house, greeted her and said, "Jesus wants you and the other women to join Him for the Passover feast." Mary invited Peter and John in, asking them to wait so they could all travel together.

Later that evening, the three women and the two men entered a large upper room where the feast was prepared. Mary, Mary Magdalene and Salome sat at a small table watching and listening. No one spoke and no one ate.

Jesus, groaning as if in pain, looked from one apostle to another. Love filled His heart for them. His gaze lingered on His mother. She was sitting with her head bowed, not wanting to meet His eyes, for she knew what was coming. Mary wanted to scream, "No! No! Do not let this happen to You!" She knew she had to be strong to endure the hell that was about to come.

Jesus got up, set aside His robe, wrapped a towel around His waist, poured water into a basin, and bent to wash His apostles' feet. John wept as Jesus washed his feet because he loved this humble man so much.

When He approached Peter, Peter said, "There is no way, Lord, that You are going to wash *my* feet."

Jesus replied, "Peter, if I do not wash your feet, you have no part of me."

"O Lord, then please wash my whole body!"

Jesus said, "The one who has washed you is clean — and you my apostles are all clean — but one."

Jesus turned, went to His mother and bent at her feet. Removing her sandals, He washed each foot, and then kissed them. He said, "Blessed is the fruit of your womb. Blessed are you among women, beautiful virgin mother." Mary reached down and touched her son's head, pulling Him close as she let the tears fall.

The Lord said, "There is nothing more pure and sincere than a mother's tears for her child."

Mary's prayers for strength and courage for her Son went straight to Heaven to God ... and the angels cried with her. When He was done, He went to Mary Magdalene and Salome and washed their feet as well. Getting up, He went back to Mary Magdalene and, bending down, kissed her on the lips. "Mary," He said, "never quit, for there is much to do in my name. I have been loved well by you, and I am honoured."

Salome, overcome by the touching scene, wept, her heart overflowing for this man. Jesus took her hand, saying, "Weep not for me, for I go to prepare a place for you. For in My Father's house there are many mansions. If it were not so I would tell you."

As they prepared to eat, Jesus said, "One of you will betray me." The apostles and the women were stunned, except for the one who was going to deliver Him to His enemies.

"It is written," said Jesus in a quiet voice — "that the Son of Man will die — but woe to him who betrays Him. It would be better if he had never been born. He who dips his hand with me in the same dish shall betray me."

Peter exclaimed, "Not so Lord! I would protect You unto death."

"Peter ... Peter," Jesus said, "before the cock crows tonight, you will deny me *three* times."

Mary held her breath as each of the apostles said, "Is it *I*, Lord?" Mary watched as Judas Iscariot left, for when Judas asked, "Is it I?" Jesus said, "You have said it, go and do what you have to do." Tears fell from Mary's eyes for she knew in her heart this would be the last time she would ever see Judas Iscariot alive.

Then Jesus took bread and broke it, saying, "Eat, for this is my body." He then took the wine and said, "Drink. For this is my blood."

Later, bidding Mary Magdalene and Salome goodnight, He retired to a garden place called Gethsemane. Mary followed with Peter and two sons of Zebedee. There was no way she could go home. Mary knew her son was going to be taken from her and she wanted to be with Him as long as possible.

Jesus said to them, "My spirit is sorrowful even unto death. Stay awake and watch with me."

Mary watched as He went away from them to pray. Falling to her knees, she prayed for her son. Her thoughts turned back to when Herod wanted to kill Him, to the time He got stung by a bee, the time He choked on her. Had He not been lost for three days in Jerusalem? Had

He not fallen into the well and almost drowned and then James went down to get Him? Mary had been so afraid they would both drown, she wept for two days. Yes, she was always frightened for her child's life and people had made her that way. Mary watched as Jesus got up and went to wake the men.

"Cannot you pray with me that this cup should pass? He asked." Jesus went back to pray and Mary knelt closer to Him. She heard Him pray, asking that this cup would pass Him by. "Let it be what you want," she heard Him say to His Father in Heaven, "not what I want."

Again Jesus got up and went to the sleeping men and said, "The spirit is strong but the body is weak." Leaving them, he again went to pray.

Mary watched as sweat ran down His face like drops of blood. He was terrified by what was to come. Mary went to her son and wiped the sweat from His face. Still on His knees, He pressed His head to her and as she held Him, great wracking sobs shook His body. When He stopped crying she knelt and prayed with Him.

The sounds of voices could be heard and Jesus got up and said, "It is time for the Son of God to be given up."

An unruly crowd came, with Judas among them. After Judas had kissed Him, Jesus said, "So the Son of God is betrayed with a kiss and thirty silver pieces."

Mary and the three apostles watched as officials dragged Him away. Being afraid, the apostles ran away, leaving Mary alone in the garden. Mary, gave the crowd time to move ahead of her, and then followed her son and His captors. They took Jesus into the courtyard, leaving soldiers to guard the entrance.

Mary ran to the servant's entrance. There were no soldiers there. Going in and staying out of sight, she found the courtyard where they had her son. Hiding behind the pillars, Mary watched as they prepared to flog Him. His arms were tied to a post above His head and they removed His clothes. Four men — big, rough men who felt no pity for the ones they flogged — were full of wine. Their intention was to beat Him to death. Two at a time, they took turns. Mary heard His groans as He writhed under their blows. When two were played out, the other two took their turn. His body was covered with black, blue, and red marks. His blood ran freely to the ground. He looked at His torturers with bloodied eyes and begged for mercy.

Mary was angrier than she had ever been in her life. The Jews had an ancient law prohibiting more than forty lashes and the Pharisees always made sure the law was strictly kept, insisting that the flogging stop at thirty-nine lashes just in case of a miscount. But the flogging of Jesus kept on and on … every time the whip came down somewhere on His body Mary winced … feeling the whip with Him.

The flagrum (or flagellum) was a Roman scourge, a short whip with several heavy leather thongs with two small balls of lead attached near the end of each. The heavy whip was brought down with full force again and again across Jesus' back. At first the thongs only cut through the skin, but as the blows continued, they cut deeper into the tissue. The extent of this produced an oozing of blood from the capillaries and veins. Finally, arterial bleeding from the underlying muscles appeared. The small balls of lead produced large deep wounds that broke open until the skin from His back hung in long ribbons. The entire area was an unrecognizable mass of torn and bleeding tissue. Mary counted the lashes as they came down on her son — ninety-two times.

The centurion came in and hollered at them to stop. He was very angry — "I told you to flog Him — not kill Him!" Throwing down their whips, they untied the unconscious Jesus from the post and He fell into His own blood. The centurion threw a pail of water on Him. "Help Him get up!" he ordered, "And put this robe on Him!"

Mary watched as they clothed Him in a purple robe and put a stick in His hands for a sceptre. They plaited a rough crown of thorns and drove it down on His head so hard that more blood ran down His face. They mocked and spit on him, and slapped his face with stiff reeds. Bowing down, they mockingly worshipped Him yelling, "Hail! King of the Jews!"

Finally, tired of their sadistic sport, they tore the robe from His back. It had stuck to the clots of blood and serum in the wounds, so when they ripped away the robe, the pain was as excruciating as though He were being whipped again. The wounds began to bleed again and they told Him to put on His garment, which was immediately soaked with blood.

Mary watched Him stagger ahead of His tormenters. Once they were gone, she stood up. Holding on to a pillar, she vomited. Never had she witnessed anything so unmerciful. She struggled down the steps to the courtyard to where He had been tied. There was blood everywhere. Kneeling down, she touched her son's blood and groan after groan emanated from her as if she were an animal. Her tears mingled with His blood.

This was the way John found her. "Mary! Mary!" he cried, as he fell to the ground beside her. "What are you doing?" Taking her in his arms he helped her up and said, "Come. We must follow."

As they came out of the courtyard they watched as Jesus struggled under His heavy cross. The procession of Jesus, two thieves, and the execution detail of Roman soldiers headed by the centurion, began its journey to Golgotha.

In spite of His efforts to walk erect, the cross and the shock of losing so much blood caused Him to stumble and fall. Mary watched as the heavy beam pushed Him to the ground. His garment came away where the cross had rubbed. Between the scourging and the cross digging into His shoulder, she saw a wound so deep it reached His shoulder bone.

Pushing and shoving through the crowd, she fell to her knees beside her son. "I love You, my boy," she whispered. "Oh how I love You!" He looked deeply into her soul. And where she had felt totally abandoned by God, she now felt a surge of hope. "I love you too, Mother," He managed to gasp, "but my time has come and you have to be strong."

Under the rough prodding of a soldier, He staggered to His feet, trying to balance the weight of the cross on His mutilated back. He walked, fighting for every footstep. Again He fell and pitiful groans came from within His body. Mary saw a bucket of water and ran to get Him a drink, only to have it kicked from her hands as she knelt beside Him. The soldier raised his foot to kick her out of the way. Jesus grabbed his foot and said, "No!"

The soldier shuddered as he looked into Jesus' eyes, then lowered his foot and snarled, "Be gone woman!"

The centurion wished for the first time that he were somewhere else, as something deep inside him ripped apart. He suddenly felt pity for the mother and son on the ground before him. Lowering his head he cried for what he still had to do. Now anxious to finish the crucifixion and put this man out of his agony, he scanned the crowd and selected a North African, Simon of Cyrene, to help Jesus carry the cross.

With one hand, Simon easily lifted the cross from Jesus, who was still prostrate on the ground. And, with the other hand, he helped Jesus to His feet. Gasping for breath, Jesus clung to Simon's clothes with the last of his strength. Simon said, "Hold the cross and I will carry it and You. Just move Your feet." Pity tore through Simon, for never had he seen a walking dead man. The man had been scourged to the point of being unrecognizable. In places the skin of his face hung in strips. The only parts recognizable were His bruised eyes. The rest of His swollen face was a bloody wound with his nose split open. It looked like He was wearing a grotesque mask.

At the top of the hill, Jesus fell and a soldier hollered at Simon to drop the cross. He kicked Jesus in the side, rolling Him onto His back. Gasping for breath, Jesus began to vomit. Simon grabbed the soldier's arm as he moved to strike Jesus with the whip. "Have pity man! He is done for! He's no threat to you!"

Slapping Simon with the back of his hand, the soldier yelled, "Stay your mouth or you will end up beside Him!" Anger washed over the big man as the soldier turned to kick Jesus again. Reaching out his huge arms, Simon grabbed the soldier, lifted him from the ground and bellowed, "So be it, but you will not kick Him again!"

The centurion, hearing the ruckus, came over to the struggling men and hollered at the soldier, "Stop! That is enough." To Simon he said, "Be on your way before you get hurt. You have done what was asked of you." Simon turned to look at the man on the ground as they dragged Jesus to the cross. He watched as they seized His right arm and placed it on the crossbeam. Holding Him down, they took a long thick nail, pressed it against His wrist, and with a great hammer drove the spike through His wrist into the wood. Simon shook his head sadly and said, "God have mercy on this man, for nobody else has." Tears filled his eyes for the suffering man.

Going over to Jesus he said, "Is there anything you want?" as they pulled His left arm to the beam. "No, go!" Jesus gasped. "You have done enough. You will always be remembered as the man who carried my cross. You shall always be remembered, for many will be called to carry my cross and will fail to do so."

Simon nodded sadly and turned away, knowing this man would soon be dead. As they drove the second spike through Jesus' wrist, Simon heard Him give a deep, guttural groan and at the same time, a woman screamed beside Him. Mary could no longer suppress the screams that came from her throat as she threw herself to the ground beside her son.

Once they had driven the spikes into His wrists they tied His arms to the cross with ropes. At the top of the cross they put a sign that read "Jesus of Nazareth King of the Jews". They flattened His knees, fastened His left foot over His right foot and drove another long spike through both feet into the cross. They dragged the cross to a hole in the ground and quickly hoisted it upwards, letting it fall into the hole. As it fell, the force shook Jesus and His wounds broke open again as His body lurched against the nails. He moaned as His muscles and bones screamed in agony.

When the soldiers moved back, Mary went to the foot of the cross and wrapped her arms around her son's bloodied legs. She held them in her arms as His blood dripped on her head from above. Jesus knew His mother was there and knew that never before in creation had there been such motherly love or greater suffering than what His mother was enduring.

Long ago she had been told that her heart would be pierced by a sword from the pain and sorrow she would endure while watching her son die ... a mother suffering with God ... who in turn was suffering for all mankind while making His Son the pure sacrificial lamb.

Mary was aware that Mary Magdalene, Mary the mother of James and John, and the mother of Zebedee had joined her at the cross. Mary cried out to the women, "How can I watch my child die in such a way? My whole body is dying with Him! His agony is mine but I know it can be only a fragment of His. And I am unable to help Him."

Even though threatened by the soldiers, Mary held on to His feet. A soldier tried to push her away, but Jesus whispered, "Let her be." The man met Jesus' eyes and fell to the ground, feeling as if he had been punched in the stomach. He felt profound shame as he got up, for he had lifted his whip to hit Mary.

Mary cried and protested at times and damned the soldiers to Hell, screaming at all those whom she felt were hurting her son. She cried but no tears came. The crucifixion of her son had become public grief as those around her watched her reaction. But she did not notice or care as she tried to protect Him from any more pain. Her body bent in agony as she mourned her son, her features dishevelled, wild, and twisted. She felt the soldiers were trying to steal her grief. The affront to humanity and to justice outraged her.

The whole earth was crying out in protest and despair as Mary watched innocence die. Darkness covered the light of day, while lightening cracked in every direction. Rain fell in torrents and the earth shook beneath their feet. It was a truly hellish moment in time.

Mary knew she must get hold of herself. But she had witnessed a horrendous and traumatic happening and to deny herself this outpouring of grief would be to deny her humanity. She cried out again, damning Herod, Pontius Pilate, and the soldiers. At times she found herself screaming at the top of her lungs. Her screeches were so piercing that the soldiers covered their ears, but still — they heard those screams — and knew that the anguished sounds came from a mother's pierced heart.

As Jesus' arms began to fatigue, great waves of cramps swept over His muscles, knotting them in a deep and relentless throbbing pain. With the cramping it became physically impossible for Him to pull Himself up. He hung in a grotesque and agonizing position as his muscles became paralyzed, making it impossible to find even momentary relief from his agony. He could still breathe in slightly but could barely exhale as He struggled to get the air out again.

As life seeped out of him, He moaned "Father forgive them, for they know not what they do."

One of the criminals dying at His side asked Jesus for forgiveness, while the other mocked Him. Jesus groaned to the one who asked for forgiveness struggling to get each word out, "Today, you will be ... with me ... in paradise."

Then, looking down from the cross, He said to His beloved mother, "Behold thy son." And he said to John, the only apostle who had not run away, "Behold your mother."

Then, after a moment of silence, he moaned grotesquely ... "My God! My God! Why have You forsaken me?" His relentless hours of excruciating pain, His torn and twisted ligaments, His indescribable cramping, and the agony He felt as each of His joints dislocated were more than even He could bear. He gasped, and with a slow and fading voice he whispered, "I thirst ..." A soldier approached with a sponge soaked in sour wine, and lifted it to His lips. Jesus turned His head away and said in a tortured whisper ...

"It is finished ... Father, Into Your hands ... I commit my spirit."

Then, to make sure He was dead the centurion drove a spear through His ribs and into His heart.

Mary His mother, beautiful in body and soul, greater than the rest of humanity, and greater in grace than the angels, bowed her head and cried. She was with Him, the Son of God, when He came into the world and she remained with Him as He left the world.

As she fell to the ground, the sun darkened even more and the veil of the temple was ripped from top to bottom. Again an earthquake shook the land and rocks shook loose. Soldiers and onlookers ran for their lives, yelling — "Surely this *was* the Son of God" — as thunder and lightning rocked the Heavens and rain fell in torrents.

John took Mary, Mary Magdalene, and Salome to a grotto to wait for the storm to lessen, telling them, "We must find help to take down His body."

As the little group came down the hill, they found Peter bent over and weeping. Mary said with great sadness in her voice, "Peter …"

Turning to look up at her, the big man threw himself to his knees in front of Mary and sobbed, "I told Jesus I would protect Him with my life. He told me that before the cock crowed three times … I would deny Him and … and I did!" The big man's body shook with sobs and remorse.

"Peter, you are sorry for your sin. For that reason my son hangs up there on that cross — but He died for all sinners — and I know He has already forgiven you."

There was a moment of silence and then John calmly said, "Come, we must take Jesus from the cross and find a safe place for Him."

As they walked, they met Joseph of Arimathaea, a rich disciple of Jesus. Greeting Mary he said, "I feared the Jews would not allow me Jesus' body so I went before Pilate and asked him. And he granted me permission. Come. We will take Him from the cross." The men began the task of taking Jesus down as Mary watched, not moving or talking. She was as a statue, drained to the heart, with no feelings during the ordeal.

Peter climbed a ladder and using a chisel, file, and hammer, he worked until the nails broke. Then he pried the nails out of Jesus' wrists and, leaving His arms tied to the cross, Peter climbed down and removed the thick spike from his Lord's feet. Mary watched his careful movements, missing nothing, as he climbed the ladder once more to untie the arms of Jesus, letting the lifeless body fall against him. Crying, he handed Jesus' body to Joseph, John, and Nicodemus, who had joined them.

Once Jesus' body was on the ground, Mary sat beside Him and Peter gently put Jesus' head into her lap. He thought his heart would break as she held her son's bloodied body close to her. He was so beaten beyond recognition, that had she seen His body elsewhere, she would not have known Him. She rocked Him in her arms and the sounds coming from her were more like a wounded animal than the calm and peaceful woman they knew. Her gentle mind had all but snapped for what she had endured while witnessing the horrific crucifixion of her son.

As the women tried to comfort her and the men waited for the intense agony to lessen in her frail body, they saw a soldier coming toward them. "What now?" Peter muttered, with a frown. "Have they not done enough?"

As the soldier came closer, they saw it was the centurion who had supervised the crucifixion. Walking past the men he knelt beside Mary. "Woman what is your name?" he asked as he put his arms around her shoulders. "Woman ... I am sorry for what was done to your son. Can you forgive me?"

Turning to him, with Jesus' head still in her lap, she pounded on his chest until she had no more strength. The big man did not move or try to protect himself from her blows. When she collapsed against him he said softly, "I do many things in the name of Rome ... and I must obey ... because I am a soldier. If I do not obey an order, it means my life. Today, woman, I am ashamed to be a soldier, for I have killed an innocent man. If you can find it in your heart to forgive me for what I have done to your son, I may be able to live with myself."

Mary knew what her son expected ... slowly and reluctantly she whispered, ... "Not for my sake, but for His, I forgive you. If I did not, it would hang Him on the cross again, for that is why He died, for the forgiveness of sins. Yours for what you did to Him and mine for the hate in my body that consumes me. Only through forgiveness can we have eternal life."

The centurion nodded, "I have something for you. Here is His robe. We drew lots for it. I won and now I bring it back to you." Then he gently laid the garment over her son, who still lay in her lap. As he slowly rose to a standing position, he said, "Woman, you gave me more than I deserve." Then bidding her goodbye he left her and the others standing on the hill.

Turning to look back at the scene, the centurion shuddered at the thought that this was what men were capable of doing to one another. He knew his job was to defend Rome, but *why* did it have to include torture and grotesque murder? And how did torture and slaughter make him a man he could be proud of? His heart saddened as he watched the small procession head down the hill carrying the body of their Christ.

Nicodemus brought a mixture of myrrh and aloes and helped Mary and Mary Magdalene clean Jesus' body once they had moved him to the opening of the tomb. As Mary washed away the blood and dirt, she wondered if they could clean His body and position it well enough for burial. She got Nicodemus to help her straighten His arms. They had been splayed out for so long in one position it was almost impossible to bring them into a natural position closer to His body.

Mary Magdalene washed His bloody matted hair. Wails of horror came from Mary's throat as she worked on the wounds of her child. The worst one was on His shoulder where the heavy cross had cut Him to the bone. There was a cut in the bone where the wood had rubbed back and forth against his shoulder while He dragged the heavy cross.

Painstakingly, Mary wrapped His body with clean linen. She then placed her hands on His head, in an attempt to cradle it to her breast. Mary was conscious of the warmth of her body against the coldness of His lifeless form. Holding Him closely she tried to breathe her life into him. For a moment, with one hard pull she held him close to her body, she felt as though she could pull Him from death to life. Then Mary felt Mary Magdalene's gentle touch and with a shudder, pulled herself from her trance.

The moment of almost giving life to her son again had felt so real — "Why? Why not!" — she cried to herself. She watched Salome, Mary Magdalene, and Nicodemus complete the finishing touches and knew then she had to let her son go.

When they were done, they helped Mary up and said, "Come. We will place Jesus in Joseph's tomb, one that he had recently hewn in the rock for himself. It honours him to give it to Jesus for His resting place."

After Jesus was placed in the tomb they led the weeping mother of Jesus outside and rolled a huge stone across the door of the sepulchre. Mary's thoughts went back again to her child. She had delivered Him in pain, nursed Him at her breast, and loved Him with her whole being and now, in pain again, she had laid Him to rest. She said, "I will never be silent about my son. I will tell the world what He taught and I will certainly tell of those who crucified Him. I will make it matter to the world to teach what He taught, for if I stay silent, it will belie everything He stood for and died for."

As they began to leave, Mary's frail body could not take any more of the pain she had endured that day, a pain that made it hurt to breathe. She crumbled to the ground. Peter scooped her into his powerful arms and carried the broken-hearted mother home. Mary Magdalene and Salome followed, their hearts breaking for the woman who had just lost her son and for the man they had left in a cold dark tomb.

Once home, the women helped Mary to bed and bought her food and drink, sitting quietly beside her until she fell into a fitful and troubled sleep.

That day had been the preparation for the Sabbath and they rested on the Sabbath day according to the Commandments. Mary' exhausted body could go no more, so she asked to be alone with her thoughts. She needed to hold her pain close to her body, as if holding a baby, afraid of sharing her thoughts and feelings with anyone, lest the bitterness show through. Her need to hide from the world was desperate.

It was late in the evening when James, her stepson, stopped by. The world was not done with her son yet. Apparently, the Chief Priests and the Pharisees had gone to Pilate to demand a guard detail at the tomb. When Pilate asked why, they told him it was because Jesus had said that in three days He would rise from the dead. "We want guards there," they insisted, "until the third day, in case His disciples come in the night and steal Him away."

Pilate listened to their case, then said, "So be it. You shall have your watch. Go your way and secure the tomb." They sealed the stone to their satisfaction, and set soldiers at the tomb to keep watch.

Mary was quiet as James told her what had happened with the Chief Priests and the Pharisees. "Yes," she said, "they fear that He will arise from the dead, but unfortunately for them it *is* going to happen. I do not suffer here by myself because I have no hope — as if I do not believe — My Jesus *will* be raised from the dead! I cry because of the hate and torture that humans can bestow on one another. I cry for my son's suffering and pain and the terrible burdens of those same people's sins on His soul. He died for the sins of the world, even for those who crucified Him. But I cry hardest because they crucified God Himself, the only one who was and is capable of loving them. Even now He forgives and loves them in spite of themselves and I am still struggling to understand how He can."

James nodded and said to the gentlest woman he had ever known, "But you do, Mother, for you know that everything Jesus taught was always with love." He went to her and kissed her, saying, "You must rest now for you will be getting up early to go to the tomb."

Mary Magdalene said, "I want you to come with me to anoint Jesus' body."

Mary nodded ... adding ... "Presuming He is still in the tomb."

Stunned, James looked at her and said, "I hadn't thought about it, but tomorrow will be the third day!"

Mary nodded, saying, "Go now James. I feel so weary. I will see you tomorrow." When James left, she went to bed, closed her eyes in prayer, and whispered, "I will see You sometime tomorrow, my Son."

Mary woke to Salome shaking her gently, "Come Mary, it is time to wake for we want to make haste to the tomb. Mary Magdalene is making us something to eat before we leave." Hurrying to dress, Mary felt an inner excitement building, even as a calming peace invaded her body. A knock on the door brought Mary, the mother of James, and Joanna who were going with Mary, Mary Magdalene, and Salome to the tomb.

As the women approached the tomb a great earthquake shook the ground, for an Angel of the Lord had descended from Heaven, rolled back the stone, and was sitting on it. His being was like lightning and his cloak as white as snow. The Angel frightened the soldiers so badly they fell to the ground, covered their heads, and cried in fear. When they realized that no harm would come to them, they scrambled to their feet and vanished past the women, running for their lives.

The Angel said to the women, "Fear not, for I know you seek Jesus who was crucified. Why do you seek the living among the dead? He is not here, for He has risen. Come! See the place where He lay."

As they entered the tomb another Angel clothed in a long white garment sat on the burial stone. "He is not here. He has risen as He said. Did He not say the Son of Man would be delivered into the hands of sinful men, be crucified, and on the third day rise again? Go quickly and tell the disciples that He has risen. Behold, He goes before you into Galilee. There you shall see Him. Lo, I have told you so."

Trembling, Mary Magdalene said to the other women, "Wait here while I run to tell the disciples to come." When Mary entered the room where the men were mourning the loss of Jesus, she said, "Weep not! Weep not! He has risen. He is not in the tomb!"

At first they did not believe her and chided her, saying, "Do not tell tales, Mary. Our hearts cannot stand the pain."

"I do not lie. Come! Jesus' mother waits for you at the tomb Peter." Peter and a few disciples ran ahead to the tomb and entered the sepulchre. To their amazement they saw the linen burial cloth folded neatly on the stone. The women followed the men into the tomb and told them of the earthquake and the angels.

Mary Magdalene, following far behind, arrived. And fear overtook her. "Did someone steal His body?" she wondered. Seeing a man in the garden and presuming him to be the gardener, she went to him and said, "Sir, did you see anyone with a body? If you did, and if you know where they took the body from that tomb over there, would you please tell me, so I can anoint him."

The man said, "Mary!" Recognition flooded over her, and she fell to her knees crying, "Master, Master," and reached out to touch him.

Jesus said, "Touch me not, for I have not ascended to My Father. Go to My brethren and say to them that I will ascend to my Father and your Father, to My God and your God."

As quickly and quietly as He had appeared, He disappeared from before the dazed Mary Magdalene. Jumping up quickly, she ran to the tomb and told them whom she had met in the garden. The men and women said, "Come, let us tell the others. We cannot believe what our eyes have seen. How will we convince those who did not see?"

Mary's heart pounded so hard she could hear it in her ears. She thought she was going to have a heart attack. All her son's and the messengers' words from Heaven had come true. The worst had happened and was now behind her. All she had to do was wait for Him to come to her.

That evening, the first day of the week, the disciples and women were gathered behind closed doors, assembled there together for fear of the Jews. They were all the more afraid, for they had heard that when the soldiers told Pilate of the angel rolling away the great stone, they were put to death. The story in the courtyard and in the city was that the disciples had overpowered the soldiers to steal the body. There was no way Pilate could let the soldiers live lest they went about and told what they had seen.

As they sat quietly in the locked room, talking of the amazing things that had happened, Jesus suddenly stood in their midst and said, "Peace be with you!" He showed them His hands, feet, and side. And to His mother He showed the terrible wound where the cross had cut into His shoulder. Jesus said, "Peace to you. As my Father has sent me, so I send you." As He said this, He breathed on them and said, "Receive the Holy Ghost. Whose sins you remit, they are remitted, and whose sins you retain, they are retained." Then after visiting a while longer Jesus took His leave and vanished as quickly as He had appeared.

Mary Magdalene, holding Mary in her arms, wept joyfully as Thomas came in. Not knowing how to accept the jubilant group and wondering how they could be so happy when he was so sad, he asked, "What is happening?" The apostles and the women told him they had seen the risen Christ and that He had been with them. Thomas, in deep disbelief, said, "Unless I see His hands and put my finger into the print of the nails and thrust my hand into His side, I will *not* believe!"

Mary was appalled that denial was coming directly from one of His apostles, one who had walked with Him. Turning to Mary Magdalene she said, "Fetch Salome and let us go home. It has been a long, long day and I am too weary to try convincing Thomas that a mother would never lie about a thing like this!"

Eight days later they were again together when Jesus appeared saying , "Peace be with you." Looking at Thomas he said, "Reach out your fingers and behold my hands. Reach your hand and thrust it into my side. Be not faithless, but believing."

Thomas fell to his knees crying, "My Lord and my God!"

Jesus said to him, "Because you have seen me you believe, but blessed are the ones who have not seen me and yet have believed. Believe, Thomas, for all power is given to me in Heaven and on Earth. I am with all of you always to the end of the world. Go and preach to all nations, baptizing with water in the name of the Father and of the Son and of the Holy Ghost. He who believes and is baptized shall be saved, but he who does not believe shall be damned. These signs shall follow them who believe. In My name you shall cast and speak with new tongues. You shall take up serpents and if you drink any deadly thing, it shall not hurt you. You shall lay hands on the sick and they shall recover."

Then, going to His mother, He took her in His arms and said, "Farewell, Mother," and kissed her. "Come now, all of you, it is time for me to leave." As Mary held her son's wounded hand, Mary, Jesus, and Mary Magdalene walked out of the room. He led them as far as Bethany. Then, lifting up His hands, He blessed them, then turned and kissed Mary Magdalene and his mother.

"Lord," Peter said, "will You at this time restore the Kingdom to Israel?"

Jesus replied, "It is not for you to know the times or the seasons which the Father has put in His own power. You shall receive the Holy Ghost and a great power. You shall be a witness to me both in Judea and in Samaria, and to the uttermost part of the earth."

When He had spoken these things they watched in awe as He was taken up and a cloud received Him out of their sight. While they looked steadfastly toward Heaven, two angels in white appeared beside them. One gently touched the crying women's shoulders and said, "All you of Galilee! Why do you stand gazing up into Heaven? This same Jesus, who is taken up from you into Heaven, shall so come again in like manner as you have seen Him go into Heaven."

Mary fell to her knees crying and worshiping God. Her son was with God, His Father, and nothing on the earth could bring Him harm again. For thirty-six years He had walked the earth in all His humanity and now He was divine.

The disciples gathered weeks later to discuss what was to be taught, what towns and countries to go to, and who was to go where to teach. The women began discussing where their journeys would take them. Mary Magdalene said to Mary, Salome, and Joanna, "I am going to go to Rome to teach, to anoint the sick, and cast out demons in the Lord's name. Much was done for me, so now I will help others to the Lord."

Peter, hearing her, said, "Nonsense! Women cannot teach, for it is against the law."

Mary Magdalene quickly replied, "I saw the Lord in a vision and He said I am privileged because I did not waiver.

For where the mind is, there is the treasure. I said to Him, 'Lord, does he who sees in a vision see it through the soul or the spirit?' Jesus said, 'He sees neither through the soul nor through the spirit but through the mind, which is between the two, and the vision is real. I promised that the pure of heart would see God. And that is a promise of bodily transformation, not just insight'. "I will explain the powers of the soul and the Spirit to you, said Mary.

The Spirit said, 'I did not see you ascending.'

The soul answered, saying, 'I saw you but you did not see or recognize me. I served you as a garment and you did not know me.' After the soul said this, it went away rejoicing greatly.

The Spirit then came to the next power, that which is called ignorance and questioned the Soul saying, 'Where are you going? In wickedness you are bound. Do not judge.'

The soul said, 'Why do you judge me even though I have not judged. I was bound; though I have not bound, I was not recognized. I have recognized that the all is being dissolved, both the earthly things and the Heavenly'.

When the soul overcame the third power it went upward and saw the fourth power, which took seven forms. The first form is darkness, the second is desire, the third is ignorance, and the fourth is the excitement of death. The fifth is the kingdom of the flesh, the sixth is the foolish wisdom of the flesh, and the seventh is the wrathful wisdom.

These are the seven powers of wrath.

They ask the soul, 'Where do you come from, slayer of men? Where are you going, conqueror of space?'

The soul answers, saying, 'What binds me has been slain, and what surrounds me has been overcome. My desire has ended and ignorance has died, I was released from the world in a Heavenly way. From this time on, I will attain silence for the rest of the time of the season."

When Mary had said all this, she fell silent since it was only to this point that the Saviour had spoken to her. Andrew said to the other disciples, "You can believe her if you wish, but I do not believe the Saviour said this."

Peter nodded in agreement with Andrew, and said, "Would Jesus speak to a woman without our knowledge? Are we supposed to turn ourselves around and listen to her, a mere woman? Did the Lord prefer her to us?"

Mary Magdalene started to cry, saying, "Peter, my Christian brother! What are you thinking? Do you think I made this up or that I am *lying* about the Saviour?"

Levi, listening to the three-way conversation, said, "Peter, you have always been hot-tempered and now I see you and Andrew contending against women as if you were the High Priests and Pharisees. If the Saviour made Mary Magdalene worthy, who are you to reject her? Jesus knows her well. That is why He loved her. Did He not tell us to preach the gospel and not to make other rules or laws beyond what He taught?"

Mary stepped forward and with a stern voice, which none of the apostles had ever heard her use, said:

"Peter, I am angry with you. Many men have been baffled and confused and scared of women since the dawn of time. Women have the power to conceive life so there is no greater power in the human race. We bring forth life and it gives us the power to love in a way no man ever can. Men are jealous and terrified of the power of that love, yet all men are born of women.

No, Peter, Jesus did not love Mary Magdalene more than the rest of us. It bothered you when Jesus would kiss

Mary Magdalene, yet you men kiss one another in greeting or in bidding one another farewell. The holy kiss is the key of Christianity, for it shows love one to another and that is what the Saviour taught. Yet when it was bestowed on Mary Magdalene, it grieved you. Do not let jealousy overcome you for no one is better than the other.

Peter, did He not tell you when you were offended by the love He had for women that He loved them as much as any man? Did He not say when a blind man and one who sees are in darkness they are no different from one another? When in the light, he who sees the light and he who is blind will remain in darkness. Was not Jesus telling you not to be blind to the love He had for women?"

Then, her voice quivering with emotion, Mary said, "Furthermore Peter, think back to the dawn of time and Adam and Eve. Was Eve not tempted, having never been tempted or beguiled before? She did not even know the meaning of sin and failure. But the man, Peter, was he tempted? He had the audacity to place the blame on God, saying the woman made him do it. The man was not tempted, the woman was. She failed the test but there is no excuse for the man failing as well. And what was his excuse for failing? The woman made him do it. And it was also God's fault, for making the woman for him. How pitiful.

So whose sin should be greater, hers or his? But for Eve's sin, men have used this excuse to beat and abuse women when in actuality men really hate themselves for this weakness.

God could have made the man bear children but again, in pity for what happened to the women, God still made women to be the mother of mankind. He went even further to bestow blessings on women, for a woman was asked to conceive and bear the Son of God. A woman was the first at the tomb and a woman was the first to see the risen Christ. Mary Magdalene was told to take this wondrous news to you. She has the same authority to heal the sick and exorcize demons as you, Peter. And you want to call her a *liar*?

This woman was formerly demon-possessed but she received healing and was repentant. She has never wavered from her path of loving the Saviour. Mary Magdalene, of all of you, was faithful to Him, not only in the beginning when things were good but when all of you, except John, deserted Him in fear!

Humiliated — crucified — hanging in torment on the cross, she was there with Him, not you. This is why the Lord, knowing her faithfulness and loyalty, appeared to her *first*. He esteemed her worthy ... over all ... to be the first to proclaim His resurrection.

Not only you Peter and Andrew, but also our newly recruited Paul who was picked by Jesus Himself to teach the Gentiles, have this attitude toward women.

You men hasten to do women a terrible injustice by telling such a lie, one that comes straight from the Devil himself — that women are not equal to men and are loved less by God and Jesus — *because* they are women!

Lastly Peter, it has to be said, was not the Son of God born of a woman? And was not the Holy Spirit the Father of Jesus?"

"Yes," said Peter, "that is so. The Holy Spirit came over you as His mother and you conceived and brought Him forth from your womb.

"Well Peter," Mary said, "you hear your own words, do you not? — And the rest of you — Hear his words too!" All nodded, but as the rest of Mary's comments fell on their ears, silence came over the group.

"So … did a man have a hand in the birth of the Christ? The Holy Spirit came over me, a woman, and I conceived the child. There was no man involved … only a woman and the Holy Spirit. How can Andrew, Peter, or any other man here think they are better or above a woman? Do others of you think you should be loved more by God or His Son just because you are a man?

We are to teach the world about love and equality and we are already in disagreement on the "status" of women. My Son did not place Himself above women, so by what right do you? My son said a man should be over his household and the protector of his family, but He also said a man should love his wife as he would his own body. So if a man loves his body that gives him no right to abuse the women of his house, only the right to love and respect them. Women should respect their husbands and not abuse their love and trust. This is what my Son taught.

I have seen and heard a lot of differences between all of you. Some I do not like. You must stop this sniping at one another. Teach what He taught you, not what you would like to make yourself feel important.

Defend women — for their lonely walk to Jerusalem — is just as humiliating and horrific as hanging Jesus on the cross over and over again. Men have crucified and will crucify women until the end of time. You have left them to walk the road to Jerusalem alone.

It would be nice to at least have unison amongst the ones who walked with Him and know the truth of what He taught."

When Mary finished she picked up her shawl and wrapped it around herself as if protecting her frail body from any more of the slaps of life. Tears falling, she walked to the door with her head held high, not looking at the ones she loved so much but felt so disappointed in. Mary Magdalene grabbed her shawl and followed Mary out.

She could not believe the contention that was coming from the very ones who had walked with her Son, nor could she believe what came from their mouths concerning women. She had spoken her piece and they could take it or leave it ... she would not be silenced ... and certainly did not have to subject herself to such controversy.

Peter and Andrew ran after them and Peter blurted, "Mary, please forgive Andrew and me. We do at times become too big for our sandals and grow swelled heads. We think because we walked with Him that we have more of a say than new Christians. Because we are men — we *do* think ourselves above women — and we think we know more than they do. As He was humbled, so must we be every day, for it does not take much for a man to think himself superior of his neighbour.

Turning to Mary Magdalene he said, "I am very sorry. I had no right to embarrass and humiliate you. Of course, you speak the truth. How could you speak anything else? I apologize for my jealousy, for that indeed is what it is.

I have no right to think the Saviour should love me more than any other and this will not happen again. Jesus steadily had to admonish me and I failed Him miserably at times. Now I have His mother admonishing me as well as Levi. This is not what I want, nor is this what He taught us to do. And I will talk to Paul about this." Then, walking over to the women, he said again, "Please forgive me."

Mary Magdalene nodded and said, "I forgive you Peter, but I think it would be best if I go somewhere else to teach. Since I have never met Paul, I think I will go to Rome. I believe Jesus wants me there so I can teach Paul about women."

The disciples laughed at her words and Levi said, "You will need your sense of humour and a gentle heart to handle him Mary Magdalene. He claims he does the Lord's work the best because he has no woman to care and contend for.

"That is very true Mary," Jesus' mother said. "But I have a very selfish thought. Look at the men who have wives and families. They teach and leave their families while doing the Saviour's work. They put in as many days and hours as Paul. They leave these women, with whom Paul has a problem, to carry on without their husbands; raising families, burying children, and scraping the day's meal together as best they can. They handle their everyday problems on their own without complaint while their husbands teach the Word of the Lord.

Whose cross is harder to carry, Paul's or a woman's? Does Paul know the true meaning of love, having never known the love of a woman or a child? Paul has a hard head. Did the Lord not have to knock him off his horse to get his attention? I think that there are going to be many knocks in Paul's life coming to him ... and one will be a woman."

As Mary said this, she knew in her heart that the woman would be Mary Magdalene. She sorrowed for the arrogant man, for in reality it is hard to be humbled by anyone, let alone a woman.

"I will miss you, Mary Magdalene," Mary said. "I hate the thought of you going alone and for what may lie ahead of you. You are a brave and daring woman. The world is big and has many dangers with Satan ahead of it all. You must be wise and careful and pray without ceasing, for harm is never far away."

Mary Magdalene hugged Mary and said, "I am not going alone. Salome is coming with me." By this time the disciples had gathered around, listening to the conversation but for having being rebuked by Mary, they held their peace about their concerns on women travelling alone. As if reading their minds, Mary hugged them and said, "They will not be alone, for my son travels with them."

Days later the women were ready to leave on their journey. It was a tearful farewell for no one knew how long they would be gone and the safety of their lives lay heavily on their souls. Mary embraced Mary Magdalene and Salome and said; "Go with God's blessing until we meet again."

Mary Magdalene turned to John saying, "Take care of our sister and mother and know that I love you for all your goodness towards us." As Mary watched them leave, she wept, for as sisters they had been through so much together and she wondered if she would ever see Mary Magdalene again.

$\mathcal{O}$nce settled in Rome, Mary Magdalene set out to find Paul. Nearly every day she heard something about him or his teachings, and she liked what she heard. He was a very brave man who never ceased teaching, despite severe beatings, stoning, or being thrown into prison. The prisons did not hold him, for with the help of angels he was delivered from them.

As Mary and Salome made their way through the busy streets to where Paul was teaching, Mary's heart pounded. She had heard much about Paul and his abruptness with women. She did not want to get off on the wrong foot yet she did not want to appear afraid of him. As they walked, Mary prayed to the Lord for courage and strength to deal with the man her Lord loved so much. When they reached the temple, Paul was teaching the crowd while the priests shouted at him. Mary watched him as he spoke. He is, she thought, probably is the most alluring and charismatic man she had ever heard speak or looked upon.

His obvious belief in what he was saying and his commanding stature convinced those around him that he truly believed what he was teaching. His fair hair curled at the nape of his neck as though the hand of an angel held it in place. Mary was mesmerized. But his ice-blue eyes only softened when he was teaching the word of the Lord. When speaking to those condemning him his eyes hardened ... and Mary hoped to never have those piercing eyes turned on her with such vengeance.

She knew Paul had been in many different countries and villages. He had been beaten and left for dead and still he continued teaching the word of the Lord. She knew he had just returned to Rome, and once again, was walking on thin ice.

As she looked at him, Mary Magdalene's heart did a flip. Never had she been so attracted to a man in this way, not even to her husband. "Lord," Mary prayed to herself, "what is this? Am I about to fall in love with a man who thinks woman are inferior? Lord, I have been around many men and have enjoyed their company and worked alongside them, even You my Lord. And I have never had this overwhelming feeling of wanting to be in someone's arms, nor have I wondered what it would be like to be kissed by one such as Paul. I should leave, for I want no part of this." As these thoughts ran through Mary Magdalene's head, her eyes met Paul's. And even as she tried to walk away, he held her with his piercing blue eyes.

Paul was talking to people and looking closely at their faces, trying to read their hearts as his message went forth. Suddenly, his world spun and faltered; for standing below him was the most beautiful woman he had ever seen. Black hair cascaded down her back, stopping at her waist. And the dark eyes looking back at him were as black as the night. Trying to pull his gaze away, he stepped back, bumping into his friend Timothy. Apologizing for almost knocking his friend off his feet, he turned to look back at the woman who had held him spellbound. She was disappearing into the crowd. He quickly said something to Timothy and ran down the temple stairs. Reaching her, he grabbed her arm and said, "Wait! Wait. Stop. Who are you?"

Mary Magdalene pulled free, feeling the heat of his hand through her garment. Its intensity shocked her. What was the matter with her head? Had she lost her mind?

Paul, realizing that she was struggling to pull away, said, "I am sorry!" and let go. A surge of disappointment shot through him when he'd felt the softness of her arm leave his hand. Looking her in the face, a ripple of awe and delight rushed through him, and he felt as though he were drowning in her eyes. Before the Lord had taken hold of his life, Paul had known many women, but never had one made such an impact on him. Women were made to have babies and for the glory of man; their place, he knew, was in the home. A good woman knew her place. What would a beautiful woman and her friend be doing here, alone in the street, without a male escort? "Where is your man?" Paul demanded, glaring at the woman.

Without flinching Mary Magdalene said, "I have but one man and His name is Jesus Christ. My name is Mary Magdalene and I teach that the Christ has risen. I heal the sick in His name and cast out demons."

Paul took a step back. "Mary Magdalene? I have heard of you from Peter. Why are you here?"

"I came to teach in Rome and to make your acquaintance," Mary said.

"Why did you run away?" Paul asked.

How could Mary tell him the truth ... that just by looking at him she had lost her mind? She was forty-three and acting like a child just because a handsome man stood before her. "I did not recognize you and thought you to be someone else," she stammered.

Paul looked at her strangely, recognizing a fib when he heard one, but decided not to call her on it. "Now that you have found me, we can make our acquaintance."

Mary Magdalene responded by saying, "This is my friend, Salome, the niece and step-daughter of Herod, the one who had John the Baptist beheaded."

Paul abruptly stopped walking and stared at Salome. "We have something in common for I am the one who killed and imprisoned as many Christians as I could get my hands on. Jesus had to knock me off my horse and blind me before I recognized Him."

As the women followed Paul back to the temple, he tried to avoid looking at Mary but his body was betraying him. He could feel her presence through his whole being as she walked beside him. Paul shook his head, trying not

Beverly Lein

to remember that he was the one who had, on more than one occasion, said that other men should be like him and have no need for a woman, that it was better not to have someone more important than the Lord on your mind. But of course if one were to fall into sin ... one should marry ... and here he was acting like a schoolboy over a woman he had barely met.

When they reached Timothy, Paul introduced the two women. He felt annoyed with Timothy, who kibitzed with the women. He asked questions, inquiring after everyone's health and at times had the women laughing. Paul was tongue-tied and felt that everything that came out of his mouth sounded stupid. Finally, he quit trying to make conversation, busying himself by gathering up things to take home.

Meanwhile Mary, watching him out of the corner of her eye, felt he was being rude by ignoring them. She sensed his discomfort and thought it was because they were taking up Timothy's time. Mary said to Salome, "Maybe it is best if we leave and come back another time."

Paul, hearing her, all but shouted, "No! We will go now and have supper. You can join us." He could not bear the thought of her leaving before he knew where she was staying ... and besides ... he wanted to talk to her a little longer.

Salome and Mary Magdalene accompanied the men to their abode even though they had to walk about two miles to where the men lodged. On the way they spoke of many things. Paul was spellbound. Here was somebody who had walked, talked, and lived with his Saviour. As he watched and listened to Mary Magdalene, he could not take his eyes off her glowing face. She became more alive, if that were possible, as she talked of her love for her Lord.

110

As they ate the supper that Timothy prepared Mary talked about the crucifixion ... the humiliation the Lord endured, the torturing of his body, His carrying of the cross, and of His mother Mary and her broken heart, and finally ... of taking Him down from the cross. She spoke candidly about the doubts she had had when she went to the tomb, only to find it empty, and then the great joy she felt when He talked to her in the garden.

Paul said, "Blessed are you to have been with Him through it all, but appearing first to a *woman*? That I do *not* understand."

Salome interjected, "If you will allow me, I will tell you why, just as Mary His mother told the other apostles. When they dragged Jesus to the cross, all the men, everyone but John ran away in fear. Mary Magdalene and the rest of the women did not. She was there when He died and she was there when they took Him from the cross. And it was a woman who was picked in the Garden of Eden to be the mother of all mankind. In the Garden ... the woman was tempted ... the man was not. Have you forgotten that the man blamed God for giving him the woman? Did not a man say *she* made him do it?"

Mary raised her hand to Salome and said to Paul, "God gave us a way out by promising a Saviour and He chose a woman to bear His Son, our Lord Jesus Christ. Now this is where it gets a little personal. God the Holy Spirit overshadowed the woman and she conceived. Is this not right Paul?"

"Yes," Paul said. "That is right."

"Well," Mary Magdalene said quietly, "it was the Holy Spirit and a woman. There was no man involved. Don't you wonder why He appeared first to a woman after His resurrection? Do you not think He loves us just as much as he loves men?"

Paul stood staring at the woman. And before he could stop himself, his hand flashed out and he slapped Mary Magdalene's face. Horrified, Mary Magdalene put her hand to her face, staring at the angry man in front of her. Timothy leapt to his feet and flew at Paul hollering, "By all that is holy! What are you doing! What have you done?" Paul, not understanding his own rage, kicked over the bench that was before him and stormed from the room.

To Mary Magdalene's credit she did not cry, but gracefully walked to where Salome's and her own cloak were hanging and said, "If I could bother you Timothy, would you guide us home?" Timothy rushed to help her with her cloak, for her trembling hands could hardly pull it around her shoulders. Salome was furious! Her beautiful brown eyes were flashing and she said, "If any man ever deserved to be flogged, that one does!"

Timothy was aghast, "I have never seen him so angry. I do not know what came over him. He has acted strangely ever since you women made his acquaintance a few hours ago. I have never seen him lose his composure, even when he has been beaten half to death."

Mary Magdalene said, "I would apologize if I had done or said something wrong but I have not. What I spoke was the truth."

Timothy replied, "I have to agree with you. But I too, have always thought that a man *was* part of the conception of Jesus. I just presumed that God is a man — But He is not! He is the Holy Spirit! — Therefore, neither man nor woman."

Mary Magdalene said quietly, "I did not say God was not *masculine*, for man was made in His image. I am saying it was not *a man* who lay with Mary but that the Holy Spirit overshadowed her. It is the Holy Spirit, not some lowly man, who is the father of Jesus. I feel pity for Paul for he walks nearby the Lord, yet he has no room for womanly understanding. It is most sad. I had hoped I could work with Paul but I think it is for the best if there is some distance between us. A man has never slapped me over a difference of opinion. If one does not agree with this *'esteemed'* disciple, only because God has granted him the power — Paul thinks he has the right to slap it out of that person — he still has much to learn. I will not be the one to teach him this lesson, nor have I any desire to do so. I will make sure that our paths do not cross again."

Timothy, leading the women through the dark streets, said, "Please. I beg of you. This is not the Paul I know! Please forgive him. There is something terribly wrong but I do not know what it is. I just do not know."

Mary Magdalene said quietly, "I *do* forgive him, for I must. I must love my neighbour as myself. All is forgiven, but I do not want to see him again, ever."

$\mathcal{M}$ary Magdalene loved the huge city of Rome. She and Salome found many people hungry for hope and taught them wherever they went in the city. When she met those who did not believe, she simply said, "I have seen the risen Christ and would like to tell you of Him." If they did not want to listen, she blessed them and went on her way, for there were many who were broken and if nothing else she could bless them.

After the encounter with Paul, she and Salome thought it best if they moved because Timothy knew where they lived and they did not want to be found by Paul. Not because they were afraid of him, they just did not want to have anything to do with an angry man. Mary Magdalene had her own reasons, for she could not understand why she felt compassion or why she was so attracted to a man who so despised her. She thought that she never would get over the humiliation of being slapped.

Sometimes at night Salome heard her crying and prayed to the Lord to bring her friend comfort and understanding for what had happened. Salome, more than anyone, knowing Mary Magdalene's loving and gentle heart could not believe that someone who taught the word of God could have done such a thing. Discussing it with Mary seemed to embarrass her. Perhaps because it forced Mary to think that her friend, one she held in such high esteem, had witnessed her being slapped and humiliated. So Salome did the best she could to avoid the subject.

Meanwhile, Paul searched frequently for the women. He heard of their work but never ran into them. He had been forgiven many sins when the Lord picked him to do His work. God had told him that he would suffer when preaching His word to the Gentiles ... and he did ... but this was a different kind of suffering. Paul had fallen in love with a woman he had only known for five hours and had driven her away during this encounter. The more he thought about what she had said, the more the truth of it became clear. "How could I have been so blind!" he asked himself again and again.

He prayed much about it, asking the Lord for forgiveness for what he had done and asking why this fact had not been made known to him before a woman pointed out this simple fact to him.

Finally, the Lord answered him during prayer, saying, "That is why I sent a woman to tell you, so you would know that they are loved and honoured as much as men."

Timothy knew Paul suffered much over the issue and asked him why he had reacted so negatively over what the woman said. Paul answered:

"Because I could not deal with my feelings! I was attracted body and soul to a woman I had just met. I felt deeply embarrassed about this. Since I put Jesus first in my life there has been no room for a woman. Suddenly, there was a woman standing before me and I could not get enough of looking at her or listening to her. I begrudged you talking to her and became jealous when she talked to you and not me.

Satan entered into me before I was aware he was there. It was not what she said that made me angry, it was the conflict within me about the feelings I felt for her. So it seemed to me that I had to push her away suddenly so I could feel safe. Now I cannot find her. I want to explain myself and to ask her forgiveness.

God has spoken harshly to me and I know I will, from now on, treat His womenfolk with the same respect I have for men. I feel as though I have fallen further than off a horse this time."

Timothy hugged his friend and said, "Thank you for sharing this with me. I knew there was something wrong but I did not know what it was."

Mary and Salome had been teaching in Rome's inner city for about a year when one day a Roman soldier rode by. He turned his horse around and came back to Salome and Mary Magdalene. Looking at Salome, he said, "Woman! What is your name? Who are you?" Before they could answer, he dismounted and said, "You do not know me?"

"No," said Salome. "I do not know you."

"I am Jon, the nephew of Tiberius. We visited your uncle Herod when I was about twelve years old. I was completely smitten with the beautiful young princess I met while I was there. We heard that you were dead, that they had found your garments in the river."

Salome replied, "I am surprised you recognised me after all these years. We have much to talk about. But first I would like you to meet my friend, Mary Magdalene."

Mary Magdalene was delighted with the good-looking man. He was tall, powerfully built, and his body armour only added to his huge stature. He had sandy brown hair and brown eyes and his lips curled up at the corners when he smiled. His eyes suggested an easy going attitude but it did not take long before you realized his eyes missed nothing — a trait some men had overlooked, thinking it was a fault — only to find it had cost them their lives. He was a Roman soldier and proud of it.

At first Mary felt uneasy talking to a soldier but in no time she felt quite at ease with him. Jon walked home with them, leading his horse and asking questions about their work and what they did. He laughed and said, "Oh! You teach the same Christ as the man called Paul."

"Yes," said Salome. "Is that a problem for you?"

"No," said Jon. "I laugh because I know of no one else in the world that can not stay put in prison. Some say angels open locked doors for him but now he is known as a Roman citizen. He used to direct the stoning of those who taught the resurrection before he became one himself!"

"Do you not like Christians?" Salome asked gently.

"I know *nothing* about them," said Jon. "I only arrest them when I am told to."

"If I may ask, what is your rank in the imperial army?" Salome asked.

Jon laughed and said, "Can you not see what I am by my attire?" Salome shyly shook her head and Jon laughed loudly again and exclaimed, "I am a centurion! I am a captain over many men." He liked the idea that Salome was not flattered by his rank or of his high position. Not only was he the nephew of the Emperor, but he was also his Uncle's favourite. Any time his Uncle wanted him back home he was free to go.

Days ran into weeks and Jon often came to visit Salome. One day when he came to visit, he said, "You must be tired of seeing me so often."

Surprised, Salome said, "Never. Why would you think that?"

"I am here every free moment I have, because I cannot wait to hear more of your teaching about this one who is called Jesus."

Mary Magdalene smiled to herself for she sensed the Lord was doing His work, that He had entered Jon's heart without any force and had quietly taken His place in the man's being.

"Salome, I have something to ask of you and Mary. My Uncle, the Emperor of Rome, has called me back. He is in Turin, his summer home, and he wants me to come home and visit my family and I was wondering something ... Would you women come with me to teach there? You will be under my protection and no harm will come to you. I would like to learn more about you Christians and your Jesus."

At first Mary was hesitant about leaving Rome for there was so much to do and the poor needed them badly, especially the lepers. There were few people who were willing to help the poor souls. Two years had past since she had seen Paul. There were times when she was in the same area but the minute she knew he was anywhere near, she had made herself scarce. Mary knew Paul inquired about her frequently because she constantly met up with mutual acquaintances that said Paul had asked about her.

Once Mary Magdalene decided to leave Rome for Turin, she decided to find Paul and tell him she was leaving. She could not understand why she felt she had to see him but she knew she could not leave without saying goodbye. It was one thing to avoid him when he was in the same city, as she felt close to him in a strange way, but to leave and never feel his presence again? She could not stand the thought.

In the morning she dressed, taking special care with her attire. As she piled some of her long black hair on top of her head, she noticed her eyes in the looking glass. They looked tired and had a frightened look. Mary Magdalene gave herself a shake. She was not afraid of him and he was not, she thought with determination, going to intimidate her again.

Mary realized that she actually loved him and that, somehow, she was going to tell him she did. And that was why she had avoided him at all costs. She had the work of the Lord to do. And having a husband, and possibly children, would indeed come first. It was not likely that she would or could become pregnant, being forty-seven, but having been a mother once she knew that to have children meant giving up your life to raise them. Jesus had given her life back to her and she was determined to serve no one but Him.

Mary felt humiliated to think that she was going to tell a man she loved him when he could not stand the sight of her. Once before, Mary had to take her leave reluctantly, because she had created a problem for him over women's matters. But this was different. She was now determined to tell Paul she had stayed away from him because she had slowly began to love him. It wasn't because she had not forgiven him for slapping her. If he really did have issues about women and their rights, it was up to the Lord to redirect him, not her. She had brought it to the Lord's attention and what to do about Paul's thinking was up to Him.

As she neared the place where Paul often preached, she heard a terrible commotion, with children and women screaming. Hurrying toward the screams, she saw that a tall stone wall had crumbled, trapping three or four children. Men and women were digging frantically. Without thinking, Mary joined them, digging wildly until her hands bled.

By the time they pulled the children out, all were either badly hurt or close to dying. Mary tried to comfort the mothers as they held their broken children. The first child, a little girl, was barely alive and had hardly enough strength to whimper. The girl's mother, having seen much death in her life, screamed to God to help her child. Mary laid her hands on the child and said, "In Jesus' name you are healed!"

Complete silence came over the crowd as she went to the three little boys who were lying close together. She was not sure whether they were alive or dead. Mary sat beside them, gently caressed each one, saying, "You are healed in Jesus' name." A great shout of joy filled the air, as the little ones started moving. And before the people's eyes, the children's wounds were healed.

Paul, who had heard the screams, stood transfixed, watching Mary heal the children. He could not believe his eyes; that the woman he loved was now before him kneeling in the dirt and rubble. For two years he had tried to find her and now, suddenly, he was once more in her presence. He said a silent prayer asking Jesus to help him handle meeting her the way He would expect him to.

As Mary Magdalene slowly got up off the ground, a hand was extended. Without looking up, she knew intuitively whose hand it was. Placing her bloodied and trembling hand in his, she was helped up to stand face to face with Paul. Without a moment's hesitation he leaned over, kissed her forehead gently and said, "I have finally found you. Come, we must talk."

Paul led her away from the noisy crowd who were still crying with joy and praising God. Seeing Timothy, he said, "I will not be around for a while. Mary and I are going to spend some time together." Holding Mary's bloody hand firmly as if she might escape and disappear, they headed away from the crowd to a garden about a mile away. Neither spoke until they arrived at the garden.

He then motioned her to a wooden bench and immediately sat on the ground in front of her. Taking her injured hands in his he began wrapping them with a cloth from his robe. "Mary, where have you been? I tried so hard to find you. I wanted to explain why I did what I did and that none of my reasons are justified."

Mary, looking into his handsome face, started to tremble. She wished now that she had not come, as she was frozen there, speechless. There was no way she could tell him she loved him.

"Mary," Paul continued, "I love you. I do not know how it is possible that I fell in love with you the minute I laid my eyes on you. Because of my feelings I did not know how to react to them or to you. I never thought I could love anyone, other than the Lord, and all these feelings that I suddenly felt for you made me think I was losing my mind." He looked up anxiously into Mary Magdalene's face. "Please ... please tell me you forgive me ... I understand if you do not think well of me. I've wanted to tell you that for so long. I wanted to tell you that I love you."

Mary pulled him toward her until his head lay against her. "Oh Paul. You were forgiven right after it happened. It was not a matter of forgiveness that I avoided you. It was because I had the same uncontrollable feelings for you. How do you tell someone you are attracted to them, that your knees go weak at the sight of them? I felt I could not even talk the day I met you ... and then for you to become so angry at my words ... I was just devastated. How could I imagine that you even *liked* me, let alone felt the same attraction I had for you?"

Holding her around the waist, Paul said, "Mary, you have to become my wife, for I cannot live another day without you by my side."

Mary gently pushed him away, stood up, and said, "Paul, I said I love you but I cannot marry you, for we both do the Lord's work. We were both chosen by the Lord to teach His word and He has never said that I should marry. He is taking me on a journey to Turin. I have prayed long and hard over this. And I feel in my heart and soul that this is where He wants me to go. He would never force me to do anything if I did not want to do it. I am sure if I insisted on staying here to marry you, he would respect my decision, but I feel He needs me somewhere else. You know His reasons are not ours. And I am sure that in your heart you know that you too, are needed elsewhere."

Rising up, Paul said, "No Mary. Do not tell me this." Taking her in his arms, he gave her a long gentle lingering kiss.

Clinging to him and letting the kiss stir all the emotions she felt for him was the only way she could show him how much she cared. Caressing her face and kissing her repeatedly, Paul was elated, as he had never truly loved a woman. He was overwhelmed at the feelings that rushed through him for this woman.

Mary, desperately trying to take control of herself, whispered, "Stop ... Paul ... we must talk, for there is much to be said."

Paul, still holding her tightly, said, "There is nothing to talk about. We are going to marry."

Reluctantly pulling herself away from his arms she said, "No Paul. I came to spend the day with you, to tell you I love you, and that I am leaving. I am going with Salome and Jon, a nephew of the Emperor. I will be leaving for Turin in two days. I do not know when I will be back or when I will see you again. But I had to come to you before I left. I had to see you one more time." Then she turned away from him, for she could not bear to see the pain in his face. "I cannot marry you."

Paul moaned, "What am I to do? I cannot live without you. What kind of life will this be? Loving you and not being able to be near you ... finding you again ... just to lose you? My heart cannot stand the pain of parting."

"Come Paul, let us spend the day together and let it take us where it may, for it will have to last us a lifetime. If the Lord wants us to be together, He will intervene. If He does not, I will be leaving. We will pray and ask of His wishes for us and He will answer. Let us not spend this precious time arguing and dividing."

The day was spent sitting and talking about their work. They prayed at intervals; at times they kissed and held each other.

Paul said, "I cannot believe that we let two years go by without each other when we could have been together."

Mary kissed him tenderly and said, "It was not God's will. If it had been, we would have been together sooner."

As evening approached, Paul took her to his home and together they made supper. They quietly ate their meal and then Paul said, "Mary, I need to go to sleep. You can sleep on my bed and I will sleep in the other room. Come, let me hold you for a few minutes."

After they had eaten the morning meal, they sat outside listening to the birds singing. Paul looked at Mary's serene face and said, "What are you thinking?"

"Peter. I am thinking about Peter."

"Peter? Why are you thinking about him?"

He just came to mind and I was wondering about him and what he truly thought of me.

"What were you thinking and what do you think he thought about you?"

"Jesus and I were always very close, even as children. We grew up together, chasing each other around. Because of our closeness, I think that Peter and some of the others might think there was something between us. That is one of the reasons I left Jerusalem, and the reason I left Mary, the mother of Jesus'.

Jesus kissed me often. It was never a secret that He loved me and kissed me. We never hid a kiss. It could be a kiss of greeting or farewell. Somehow, it caused jealousy among some of the disciples and gossip started."

"I knew nothing of this. Maybe Jesus knew their feelings but, most certainly, I did not."

"After Jesus died, He appeared to me in a vision and I shared this with the apostles. At first, Andrew and Peter did not believe me. They said, 'Why would He appear to *you*, a mere woman, and not to one of *us*? Or all of us!' It was a sad night, for they greatly upset His mother Mary and she had words with them."

Paul whispered, "How could they think of you like that when they knew you so well?"

"Apparently, clear heads were not among them and it does not take much to get gossip going, replied Mary Magdalene. And it is always hard to find the ones who started it. It is human nature to believe the worst about others. Usually, it is the ones closest to us that we malign the worst. I was surprised by their reaction. I believed that anyone who claimed to know God would know that Jesus never had a woman or took a wife ... for He *is* God. God cannot sin. Even as Jesus walked with us, He was God. As our Creator he would not commit incest with us, his children "

"I must speak of this with Peter," said Paul with determination. "It has gone far enough, and it sounds as if their idle speculation has greatly upset you."

Mary reached over, kissed his lips, saying, "Not as badly as the world branding me a whore because Jesus cast seven

Devils out of me. I guess when someone is possessed; the first thing that comes to people's minds is that one has to have left adulterous behaviour behind one! But I was a simple child of God — and when my whole family died — I was broken. My faith and my spirit, passed with them. How gleefully the demons entered me. It was easy for them and they were pleased to have a child of God in their hands. I was so broken I did not even know they had entered me.

"People said I did many crazy things when I was possessed, and that vile mutterings came from my mouth. They told me later I that I had refused to eat, that I threw myself off rocks or into water or fires. But no one ever said — nor even hinted — that I was wanton or promiscuous. Maybe there was a part of me that would not allow it. I do not know.

I attacked people if they approached. I remember being captured, washed, and forcibly cleaned. They tried to feed me but they eventually had to free me for I only hurt myself more while being bound. I thank those brave people who tried to help me, a stranger possessed. May God bless them.

"Many have told me I had a filthy mouth and it appalled them to hear me curse them and curse God. I remembered nothing, only the day my children and husband died.

"The next thing I remembered was that I awoke with Mary feeding me. Jesus had found me and cast out my Devils."

Paul reached over and kissed her again. "You have experienced much suffering, but we have work ahead of us and I am sure there is more suffering ahead for both us."

Mary, looking at the sun overhead reluctantly said, "Paul, we must go, for I have to prepare for the trip and I have to help Salome."

"I am sorrowed the thought of the possibility of never seeing you again," Paul whispered as he took her in his arms. "How can I let you go?"

Mary held him close, and said, "We must leave it in the Lord's hands. If we are to meet again this side of Heaven, it will be done."

When they arrived at Mary's home, Paul said, "So this is where you lived all this time. I did not know."

Mary nodded, saying, "Yes, it has been a good home."

Salome was shocked when she saw Paul. At first she was cold towards him but when she realized his love for Mary, her heart melted.

When Jon arrived and met Paul, there were a few uncomfortable moments before Jon said, "Tell me. How did you escape from prison the last time?"

"I will keep *that* a secret," Paul laughed.

"Good" said Jon ... "because if you say it was an angel ... I can never pass it on. The last soldiers who passed that story on were flogged within an inch of their lives."

"Then I will not tell you for I do not want anyone flogged," said Paul.

Jon looked into Paul's riveting eyes and immediately liked the man, knowing somehow that it *had* been an angel that freed the man from prison. He said, "Since I am a Roman soldier, there are some things I should not know, for if I did, I would have to do something about it. Let's pretend I do not know you are of those religious fanatics who agitate the Roman Empire. Let us just say we are friends."

Paul said, "I am sorry I agitate the Empire. That is not what I like to do. I only want to preach that the Christ is risen. It upsets many, of course, but most of all my own Jewish tribe."

"So you are taking the women to Turin with you?" Paul asked.

Jon replied, "Yes, are you coming to say goodbye?"

Paul looked at Mary Magdalene and said, "Yes, I will be here, for it will be a long time, if ever, before I see this woman I love again."

Jon looked from one to the other, feeling that something was not right, but he did not know what it was, and remained silent. It did not take as long as they thought to pack their belongings. Setting aside the things they would need to ready themselves in the morning, they were done in good time. Jon and Salome went to say goodbye to some friends and Mary and Paul found a huge tree to sit under. They did not talk. They just sat close together holding hands, for there was nothing left to say. Each knew of the other's love and that, before long, they would part.

Around midnight Paul said, "I must go home now, it is getting cold."

"No," said Mary, come to the house and we will stay by the fire till morning."

They went in and put some more wood on the fire. Mary got a blanket and wrapped it around both of them. Then, staring at the fire, they fell asleep and knew no more till the cock crowed and woke them. "My," Mary said, "the night passed so quickly. It seems as if I just closed my eyes." Paul hugged her, knowing what she meant.

By the time they had washed, Salome was up and fixing the morning meal. It was not long before Jon appeared with an escort and a small wagon into which they loaded the women's meagre belongings.

As Paul helped Mary and Salome into the wagon, Mary stroked Paul's face and said, "Remember, I will always love you."

Paul walked beside the wagon until they reached the outskirts of the sprawling city. Stopping, he watched the wagon until it was out of sight, and then slowly turned, and with a lump in his throat he went back to the city and his work.

❦

When they arrived in Turin, Jon took them to his family home and as they approached the huge flowing home with its balconies, Mary said, "You call this a house? It is a mansion! I have never seen anything so splendid!"

Servants ran to greet them, then helped the women off the wagon, took their belongings, and swiftly disappeared into the house. A woman of about sixty ran toward them crying, "Jon, Jon! It has been so long!" Grabbing the woman into his arms, Jon kissed her and said, "Mother! It has been four years. It surely has been a long time. I am so glad Uncle ordered me home."

Unknown to his mother (Unus), his father (Hans) had gone to the emperor and told him that his wife was crying at night, because she missed her son. When the Emperor realized the length of time Jon had been gone, he said, "Why did you not come sooner? Unus should not be without her son for that long. If I do not know what is going on in my family, there is nothing I can do, but if someone tells me there is problem, I can help."

Holding his mother in his arms, Jon reached out to his father who grabbed him in a powerful hug. "Hello son. It has been a very long time. Come. Introduce us to your friends. What lovely women!"

Mary knew she was going to like these people, as they hurried around making their guests feel as comfortable as they could.

Jon had seven brothers and three sisters and they in turn had big families. Jon was the fourth child. They were loving and respectful to and of each other and all of them lived in the area except one brother, the oldest, Taurus.

Mary and Salome immediately noticed that they were not Christians for they had different types of Roman idols here and there around the house. When given a large room to share, they immediately removed the idols and summoned Jon to take them away. Laughing, Jon said, "They are our gods. They do not bite."

Salome said, "We know that, but our God is a jealous God and there are no other gods before Him and we are not to worship craven images."

Jon replied, "I still have much to learn about this Christ of yours."

The women settled in nicely and in their own way they taught their hosts about Jesus. At times they noticed sceptical looks when they told of a miracle performed and at other times they heard the family making jokes at their expense. "Whoever heard," someone chuckled, "of anyone being resurrected from the *dead*? They are nice ladies but maybe they listen to too many tales."

Apparently, the family was rather intertwined with the Emperor as many business trips and family visits were conducted in and out of the palace. There was a pagan holiday coming up and the servants were getting ready for family and many visitors.

Mary Magdalene and Salome pitched in to help. When they had time free they went each day into the city to preach about God's kingdom. They had fun with the servants as well as family members and as they scurried around, they taught the word of God, about Christ dying for the sins of the world, and about the crucifixion and Christ's resurrection. Soon everyone in the household could tell these stories as well as the two women.

Finally, the great day arrived, and with it much excitement. The family, dressed in their finest attire, looked wonderful. Amongst the family members expected was Jon's oldest brother, Taurus, who lived the furthest away. He had seven children; the oldest a seventeen-year-old daughter, then all boys until the baby, a girl of three was born. She was the apple of her father's eye and was doted on by her siblings. According to her grandmother, she was as beautiful as a shining star. And when Mary finally met the little one, she had to agree.

Jon's mother waited with great anticipation, for she had not seen her oldest son and family for over a year. When they arrived, everyone was overjoyed to be together. Mary Magdalene and Salome were introduced and Mary immediately felt an animosity from Taurus, who stated, "Yes, I have heard of you ... and the uprising your cult started in Jerusalem. It was not stopped until their leader was crucified. I, for one, do not have time for your nonsense and storytelling. I do not mean to be rude, since you are Jon and my parents' guests, but I would appreciate it if you kept your distance from me ... and my family."

Mary said, "Very well. As you wish. We will not bother you or your family."

Unus came to the rescue, saying, "Son, that is not called for!"

"I am sorry, Mother, but I do not believe in beating around the bush. This is how I want it." Taurus was big and very handsome —one could tell he was accustomed to giving orders — and being obeyed.

When he finished speaking, his wife Sena, a beautiful woman who had stayed back with the children, approached him. "My lord, our child is very sick. You must come." Taurus immediately followed his wife. Little Nudia had been running a high fever for the last couple of days and the long trip had been hard on her.

When time for the evening meal came, Taurus and his wife were late. Because of his obvious contempt for Mary and Salome, they were seated furthest from him at the long dinner table. As Taurus and his wife entered the room they were greeted by the huge family, who all inquired how little Nudia was feeling. The family was distressed as they heard of the child's sickness and that her life was in danger. They had no sooner started supper when one of the caregivers entered the room and asked for Taurus, saying that child was dying. Taurus and his wife Sena were being summoned to come at once. As they hurried from the room, Jon said to Mary, "Come. You are needed."

Jon, knowing the women the longest, was well aware of Mary's healing powers, just as he was fully aware that he had become a Christian in his heart. He believed in the women and the story of Jesus and, in his inner being, had accepted Jesus as his Saviour.

As they entered the child's room, Taurus was on his knees beside the bed begging her to fight to live. He was sobbing as he held her small body. He cried out, "Do not die child! Do not die! I love you so much." Mary Magdalene's heart wrenched and she felt an overpowering sorrow for the huge man with the broken heart. She knew how he felt, for as she watched him, she recalled the terrible pain that had become part of her when her babies died. She approached Taurus with Jon and said, "Taurus, I must break my word and come near you and your child. Give her to me. I have the power of the Lord Jesus Christ to heal her." Taurus held the child closer and hollered at Mary to leave.

Jon stepped close to his brother and whispered in his ear, saying, "This woman is your child's *only* hope! What do you have to lose except your foolish pride?"

Taurus looked down at his daughter gasping desperately for air. Each breath was faster and shallower as her life ebbed. With an agonized groan he shoved the child into Mary's arms. She took the small hot body and said, "Taurus, do you believe she can be healed? Do you have any faith in a higher power?"

"No!" he exclaimed hotly. "I do not!" Jon stepped forward, placed his hand on Mary's shoulder, and said, "But I do Mary. I believe that the Lord Jesus can heal her."

Mary nodded and looked at the listless little one draped over her arms and knew the child had taken her last breath. She said, "I heal you in the name of Jesus Christ our Lord God and Saviour. Be well!" The child remained motionless in Mary's arms as the screams of her desolate mother and the rest of the women filled the room. Taurus, reaching for his child, cursed and yelled at Mary to get out.

Shaking her head and pulling back from the enraged man, Mary said, "But for your brother's faith your child would stay dead." Instantly, the little girl gasped weakly and jerked violently in Mary's arms, then took a deep breath, and then a deeper breath as air circulated in her body once more. The blueness of her little body was soon replaced by a normal healthy pink colour. She opened her eyes and looked bewildered at all the anxious adult faces staring down at her.

Seeing her father's face, she gasped, "Papa." Gently passing the child to Taurus, Mary quietly left the room, while great rejoicing was taking place. Salome hugged Mary and exclaimed, "He is alive and He is well!"

Mary smiled saying, "Very much so. He *is* the risen Christ."

The family was still in awe. The child had no fever and was breathing normally. The high temperature she'd experienced had not harmed her brain. She simply told her father that she was hungry. For the past four days the child had eaten nothing and her mother could barely get her to sip water. Now, unbelievably, all her symptoms were gone. Fifteen minutes earlier they had all witnessed her death ... but now before them was the same child alive and healthy ... as though she had never been sick.

Taurus turned to Jon and humbly hugged him while whispering, "Thank you, Jon, thank you for having this faith. What is it? You must tell us so we can learn of it too."

Jon smiled replying softly, "It is a grace that God the Father gives us. It is not something you learn or earn, but is given freely by His Son Jesus Christ, the risen Lord. Mary Magdalene or Salome will teach you, for they were there, with another friend Susanna and the Lord's mother Mary, when He died in Jerusalem. It seems all the men ran away except for one named John. I only know what I have been told. These two women have great power, the same as the apostles they previously travelled with. I try to remember all the apostles' names but many elude me. But I will learn more and now my mission in life is to meet them. I want to be among men who have no qualms about dying for a man they believe in."

Word of the healing of Taurus' daughter reached Emperor Tiberius and he called for an audience with Mary Magdalene. This great emperor intimidated her, but she carefully selected a humble gift and went bravely forth. The palace was gorgeous; never had she seen such riches, such grandeur, and such huge white marble columns.

When she stood before the Emperor Tiberius, he said, "Are you the one they call Mary Magdalene?"

She nodded, for no sound could escape her trembling throat. She felt the perspiration trickle down her forehead and her neck. "I *am* Mary Magdalene," she managed to say, lifting her head courageously to look the emperor in the eye. She flinched ... because he was very intimidating. His brown hair was cropped closely and Mary thought his eyes would also be brown but they were a very dark blue. He was tall and powerfully built, with a no-nonsense attitude that radiated from him. And those incredible dark blue eyes looked straight into Mary's soul — without a trace of warmth.

Mary timidly approached, holding out her right hand. It had an egg in it, which according to tradition, symbolized life. She gave it to him and said, "Christ is risen." The Emperor was not surprised with the humbleness of Mary's gift, for he was familiar with ancient eastern customs, but her greeting startled him.

Having aroused his curiosity, Mary began preaching about the resurrection and Christ's teachings. Mary told Tiberius that in the Province of Judea, Jesus the Nazarene, a holy man and a maker of miracles rose from the dead, powerful before God and all mankind. She told him Jesus had been executed at the instigation of the Jewish high priests and the Pharisees, and that Pontius Pilate had upheld the sentence.

Tiberius threw back his head and began laughing. When his mirth subsided, he mockingly said to Mary, "Woman! No one can come back from the dead! No more than this egg in my hand can turn red!"

And then — miraculously — the egg began to turn red.

He jerked his hand in surprise and the egg spun toward the floor, but not before Mary reached out and deftly caught it. Then, without a trace of a smile, she handed it back to him. Tiberius felt himself trembling inside. He had never felt fear and he had never been intimidated by anyone. What had just occurred must have an explanation. He was not a stupid man. Nor would he have lasted as the emperor or as a great leader of men if he had been.

"Woman," he commanded, "you will stay here and teach me about your Christ."

Thus, Mary and Salome stayed in Turin for two years. They lodged at the palace and had the freedom to come and go as they pleased. Things were not always pleasant at the palace, for Tiberius had to travel back and forth to Rome where there were always many problems. He was a dangerous and angry man. And not above using his quick temper on the men he had put in power. His servants said it was because he still mourned the loss of a son who had died in the year 23.

Jon came often to visit Salome, as he wanted to marry her; but Salome always told him, "If I marry you I have to be committed to you and I will not be able to come and go to teach what I feel and believe. My life belongs to Jesus. He has not told me He wants to share me with you. And, *if* we were married, I do not know if *you* would share me with Him.

Let us pray about it. I know He will answer. When? I do not know. Ask your family to pray for us as well." She could freely ask this of him because over the past two years his family had become Christians. After Jon's niece had been bought back from the dead, most of the family who had witnessed the miracle had eagerly given themselves to the Lord. Salome hugged Jon and said, "Do not be sad, we will know soon."

She was wrong. There was no answer for over a year. Then one day Mary Magdalene approached Salome and informed her that she had had a vision from the Lord concerning her.

"Come sit, Salome," Mary said. "I have words from the Lord concerning you and Jon. The Lord said that you should marry. You and Jon will have much work to do, for He is sending you to Persia, very far in the east, to preach the gospel. Do you remember when Jesus was born, the Magi who came to worship Him were from that far country? You will only have yourselves there, for the Lord has closed your womb and no children will be born to you. But you will work with the many children who need you and Jon. But you will not be alone in your old age. You will have many caring people to look after you."

That evening Jon told Tiberius that Salome and he were going to marry. Tiberius congratulated both of them, and then sent servants to fetch Jon's mother and father so they could all celebrate together. As the evening wore on, Mary requested permission to speak to Tiberius. The emperor agreed and Mary was ushered into his presence. "Mary, come. You know I love talking with you. What is on your mind?"

Once settled, Mary said, "Lord, I too will be leaving Turin. I want to return to Rome to teach. I have a friend there called Paul. I have spoken of him to you. He teaches the Gentiles the word of God. I have not seen him for nearly three years and I want to spend time with him before going to Ephesus to visit Mary, Jesus' mother."

Tiberius replied, "Mary ... I will miss you and your teachings. My whole household is now full of Christians. Is there anything I can do to honour you in some way?"

"Yes," Mary responded quietly, "could you remove Pilate from Jerusalem?"

Tiberius pondered and then said, "And where would you have me send him, woman?"

Mary Magdalene thought about this, and then answered, "You decide where you want him. I just do not want to return to Jerusalem and be afraid again. He is a most cruel leader and the Christians greatly fear him and his wrath."

Tiberius was quiet for a while, and then said; "I know the perfect place for him. Gaul! There are always uprisings and battles there. It is the perfect place for Pilate."

And so it was that Pilate was sent to Gaul to quench the fighting and disruption. And the last years of his life were filled with war and strife. A few years later Mary heard Pilate had suffered a horrible sickness and an agonizing death.

Two years after that Mary Magdalene learned that Tiberius, who gone back to Rome, had become demented. He had left control to the Senate and other scheming people. When he realized he had been betrayed, he became vengeful and mean, and lost all traces of anything Christian in his being. After some time, Mary heard that one day, while throwing a fit, he had fallen dead. Saddened by this, she hoped that in death he might find peace. She knew he had not found it in life.

When Mary returned to Rome to find Paul, she was filled with dismay because two weeks previously he had left to travel to Jerusalem to meet with Peter. Mary did not stay in Rome but made her way to Ephesus. She had not seen Mary, Jesus' mother, for five years. She had missed her deeply and often wondered how she was. Mary had to be at least fifty years old, Mary Magdalene thought. How the years flew by, with so many things happening in her life. Now she just wanted to get home to Mary.

When Mary Magdalene met Mary, she was shocked at how much her dear sister had aged. Always a small woman, she seemed even smaller and so very frail. Frightened, Mary Magdalene asked, "Mary, do you not feel well?"

"Oh yes," Mary replied. "I am just tired and the day does not seem long enough to get all the work done."

"I am here to help you now," Mary Magdalene said. "It will make things easier and you can rest more."

A year went by and the women were happy to be together again. Eventually, Mary said to Mary Magdalene, "I wish to return to Jerusalem to live. I would like to be near the tomb where my child rose from the dead. Will you come with me?"

"Of course," Mary Magdalene replied. "I would love to go back to Jerusalem." The two Mary's were occupied with the move itself. And John, who lived nearby, helped with the long journey.

By the time they were completely settled in Jerusalem, a whole year had gone by and Mary Magdalene noticed more and more how fatigued Mary was. One day, she said, "Mary, dear sweet sister, do you not feel well?"

Mary replied, "Some days I feel very well and on others, I feel so worn out."

"My dear sister, you must take things a bit more easily. You are not going out about the country and town to teach and heal. It is too hard on you. All that walking belongs to younger legs and there are enough of us to take up your duties. You work all day then in the evening you go to the tomb of Jesus. It is *too* much. From now on, all you are going to do is keep the house and I can help with that. You can go as often and as long as you wish to the tomb and you do not have to rush. Enough is enough! If you keep going at this pace, you will become very ill."

Mary was glad that Mary Magdalene was making these decisions and she was happy to comply and to limit herself to housework. The rest of her time was spent at the tomb where her son had risen from the dead. She burned incense and prayed that the Christ she had given birth to would return to her.

The Jews, however, watched her every move as she lingered by the sepulchre, and reported her to the Chief Priests. They summoned the guards and told them not to let her pray to there.

Mary felt hurt and angry and cried bitter tears to think that, as always, evil had its way. This time she was not going to be bullied or threatened. She decided she was going to the tomb even if they locked her in prison. Mary returned the next morning and as she approached she saw the guards, waiting patiently in front of the tomb. She walked boldly up to them but could not understand why they were not stopping her. To her amazement, she realized that God was not allowing them to see her. The Jews had seen her on her way to the tomb to pray. But ... once she was there ... no one could see her.

Angered and full of hate, they rushed back to the procurator, crying out that this woman and her son had ruined the Nation of the Jews. "Chase her away or we will report it to the new Caesar, Cornelius!" they threatened.

The procurator replied, "Write to him if you so wish, for I will not bother this old woman. She mourns the death of her son as any mother would."

"She does not mourn her son's death!" one of them screamed. "She celebrates His resurrection!"

Their demands eventually reached Cornelius. This was a different Caesar; for the one Mary and Salome knew had been replaced by another. Even though he had never met Mary or Salome, he knew well the many stories about them and of the healing of little Nudia. He sent an order to Jerusalem saying that no harm was to come to this woman. His dictate decreed that she was to be allowed to visit the tomb whenever she wanted — and that anyone who harmed her — would be put to death.

Mary, hearing the news, fell to her knees praising her God and Son, scarcely believing that God was using a heathen to protect her.

As the weeks went by, Mary Magdalene continued to fret over Mary. The liveliness in her step was gone and every day she seemed more than just a little tired. "Sister," Mary Magdalene asked one morning when Mary was late coming to breakfast, "stay home and rest this morning. You look so pale."

Mary, holding her head in her hands, conceded, "I will. I did not sleep last night."

Mary Magdalene said gently, "Go back to bed and I will bring you some hot milk and bread." As Mary stood, she swayed as if to faint, but Mary Magdalene quickly put her arms around her and helped her to bed. Tucking her in, she felt Mary's forehead and said, "You have a fever. You are not well."

When Mary Magdalene left to heat the milk, Mary began to pray, saying, "Lord Jesus my Son. Hear my voice and send to me the Apostle John and the rest of the Apostles, from whatever part of the country they may be." While she was still praying, the Holy Spirit picked up John in a cloud from Ephesus and set him down in Mary's room.

Surprised, John said, "Hail, mother of my Lord. Rejoice that in great glory you are going from this life." Mary peacefully replied, "Glory to God that He has brought you to me. Remember Jesus' words when He said to you, 'Behold thy mother' and to me, 'Behold thy son'?"

John went to her side and lifted her into his arms, saying, "Lord, You who have done wonderful things, now do a wonderful thing for this woman who brought You into the world. Let Your mother depart from this life with all the dignity she deserves. You promised her that You would come for her when she was to depart. Before You ascended to the Heavens ... You promised that You would come with a multitude of angels and all Your glory ... to take her home."

Immediately, a voice came from Heaven, saying, "All the apostles will come together. I, the Holy Spirit, will bring them together from the ends of the earth by way of the clouds." Instantly, the Holy Spirit appeared to the apostles near and far, saying, "I am taking you on the clouds to the side of Mary. Her departure from this world is at hand and she awaits you." Then, lifted by the clouds, they found themselves at Mary's bedside.

Mary Magdalene, entering into Mary's room, dropped the bread and milk she was carrying and cried, "What is at hand?" Hurrying to Mary's side, she saw that all the apostles, Paul included, were there.

"What? Where? ... Where?" she stammered, ... "Where did you all come from?"

Paul said, "Hello Mary. Do not be frightened, for the Holy Spirit brought us here by the clouds, for Mary requested our presence. No one is more surprised than we. Praise the Almighty God our Father."

Peter walked over to Mary and said, "Fear not, nor grieve, mother of our Lord and Saviour; for God, the Lord to whom you gave birth will take you from this life with glory." Mary took Peter's hand and said, "I am ready to depart from this life now that you have come to me by way of the Lord."

As she spoke, there appeared a multitude of angels and the Lord with them in great power. A stream of light came to Mary, as a host of angels fell to their knees and adored Him. The Lord said to Mary, "Mother, grieve not but let your heart rejoice for you have found favour and grace to behold the glory given to me by My Father. Behold, Mother, your precious body will be transferred to paradise, and your soul to the Heavens to the treasures of My Father."

Mary whispered to Jesus, "Lay Your hand on me O Lord, and bless me." As Jesus gently touched her head, she took His wounded palm, kissed it, and said, "Oh, how I have longed to do that. My dear, dear son ... How I have missed You!"

A sob escaped from Mary Magdalene as the beauty and glory of the moment overpowered her. Jesus turned to her and said, "Do not weep, sister, for soon enough we will all be together and you also will have a place in paradise."

The apostles sang a hymn and as they sang, Mary's face shone brighter than the sun in the great light of her son, as He lifted her into His arms. "Come, Mother. It is time to go." The apostles watched as the Son of God departed with His mother. The room was filled with an ineffable light and the scent of perfume lingered as they disappeared.

Everything had happened so fast. Mary Magdalene fell to her knees, crying, and praising God at the same time. Paul helped her up and said, "Weep not woman, for you have been promised paradise." Holding her, he kissed her head and said, "God bless you woman, for God Almighty has opened my heart and eyes again. The love of Jesus Christ for His mother shows me that God intended women to be equal with men, just as the Jews are to be honoured equally with Christians. There is neither Jew nor Greek — there is neither slave or free, male nor female — for we are all one in Christ Jesus. Let us therefore no longer pass judgment on one another but instead, resolve to never put a stumbling block or hindrance in the way of another. Let us welcome one another as Christ has welcomed us, for the glory of God."

Still weeping, Mary replied, "God bless you Paul, for you are truly a good man and I love you so much." Peter said with a sly smile, "Am I to marry you two?" Paul and Mary nodded in unison. "Yes," said Paul. "It is time."

With the apostles standing with them, Peter married them in the sight of man and God, ending the simple service by saying, "What God has joined together, let no man put asunder."

When finished, he asked them where they would be going to teach and Paul replied, "Back to Rome, for I am to die there." Peter nodded and said, "I too will return to Rome, for my destiny is linked with yours."

Mary gripped Paul's hand and said, "I will be at your side until the end. Together we will serve the Lord. I know your time is short, but whatever time is left, I will be by your side."

Paul nodded and said, "So be it, sister of the Lord," and he leaned down to gently kiss her lips.

Afterword

Paul was executed in AD 64 during Nero's reign in Rome. He was likely in his late sixties. Mary Magdalene died a few years later and was transported to Heaven in the arms of angels who sang songs of triumph, as they bore her Heavenwards surrounded by a great light.

No known marker or tomb reveals the place of the Virgin Marys' burial.

A Note to the Reader

$\mathcal{J}$ loved working on this story, reading the Bible to find the places and miracles, and doing research on the Internet to check the lives of the two Marys. Frequently, some of the things described by writers on the crucifixion had me tears.

Mary, Jesus' mother, never had a voice concerning her son's crucifixion. So being a mother and a grandmother, I decided to give her one. I took my own emotions and gave them to her. And I gave her a voice — one that speaks out on the historical mistreatment of women by religions, by societies, by organizations — and by men in general.

I believe that Mary Magdalene too, was not only ill-treated by the men of her day, including the apostles Paul and Peter, but by popes and religious leaders throughout history. So I gave her a voice and a chance for Paul to redeem himself, not only by falling in love with her, but being able to apologize to all women for some of his clumsy and ill-suited words.

I am sure that if Paul was still alive and could see the great harm he has brought to women ... by insinuating that we are not as equal or as loved by our Creator as men are ... he would fall to his knees and beg our forgiveness.

Somehow, widespread abuse against women *must* stop.

I hope that one day a woman becomes pope and makes sure that every woman enjoys the same rights as men, the rights that Jesus Christ gave to all of us. After all, The Bible tells us that we are *all* accountable for our sins.

Nowhere did Christ prohibit women from teaching, healing, or being heard. The Bible is full of the marvels bestowed on women. In my opinion, the most incredible marvel is that *a woman* ... bore and gave life ... to the Son of God.

All men, whether they like it or not, are nurtured and protected by women for nine months. They are, almost always, loved and protected until they become men. It is well documented that many mothers have given their lives for their sons and their daughters (who are just as much loved by their mothers as are the sons). The abuse of women, both verbal and physical, was not started by women ... but by men ... who did not know the true meaning of love.

Please remember that this is a fictional love story. I do not want people believing for a moment that Paul and Mary Magdalene married. Clearly, that is *not* a historical nor a Biblical truth.

Beverly Lein, Author

About Beverly Lein

Beverly Lein was born in Canada, in the northern town of Manning, and grew up in nearby Sunny Valley on her father's farm near the mighty Peace River.

Beverly's many jobs consisted of running her own confectionary, clerking, managing the Shell bulk station along with her husband Carson, grain farming and farming elk.

Farming elk prompted Bev's first book *An Elk In The House*, published in 2006 by Newest press in Edmonton.
A true story that has one laughing one minute and crying the next.
Her next book *The Three Saints Of Christmas* was published in 2009 By Inkwater Press from Portland, Oregon. It is a must read for all readers of all ages that believe in miracles, saints, angels, and Santa Claus. In this adventurous and compelling fictional story it takes Santa, Gabriel and St. Joseph to get a family all together for Christmas in 1866.
To the Saint's credit they do well, but to their surprise they find looking after five children a bigger job than they could ever have imagined.

Her third book *Wolf Spirit The Story of Moon Beam* was published in 2010, again by Inkwater Press from Portland Oregon.

This fictional adventure is about a ten year old girl's struggle for survival. A pack of wolves, and her loyal black horse accompany her in this struggle.

She finds love with an Indian chief, but they clash because of their cultural differences.

This book is a must for anyone who likes fast-paced drama, wildlife and romance.

As a mother of two and grandmother of five, Bev honed her natural-born storyteller's instinct on those around her.

She still spends many late nights and pre-dawn mornings writing her thoughts, fantasies, and story lines.

Her grandchildren are her sounding board and her avid critics, but most of all her greatest fans.

Bev's wild and adventurous stories are timeless, and they appeal to young and old.

What makes Beverly, her editor, and other professionals around her, especially Inkwater Press, confident that her book are relevant to you her readers?

In her own words:
I have been a avid reader of fiction since I was eight years old.

With no electric lights in our remote farmhouse, books were read in semi-darkness or with a flashlight. My mother insisted that I was going to go blind reading in the dark.

When my tasks were left undone my books were taken away from me. As a child who was sometimes deprived of books for various reasons, I created my own stories in my head and continue to do so in writing today.

I love being off on an exciting adventure in my own little world.

I am still at my age amazed that I can still pick up a book and get hopelessly caught up in it.

Whenever I buy a new book I turn back into that kid again and I am just as excited as I was back then.

My biggest dream is to share these feelings of wonderment and adventures with all of you

Bev

CPSIA information can be obtained at www.ICGtesting.com
Printed in the USA
237687LV00004B/3/P